SCRIPTED MURDER

THE SCREENWRITER AND THE DETECTIVE:
BOOK 1

E. R. FALLON

K. J. FALLON

Copyright (C) 2020 E.R. Fallon and K.J. Fallon

Layout design and Copyright (C) 2020 by Next Chapter

Published 2021 by Next Chapter

Edited by Elizabeth N. Love

Cover art by Cover Mint

Mass Market Paperback Edition

This book is a work of fiction. Names, characters, places, and incidents are the product of the author's imagination or are used fictitiously. Any resemblance to actual events, locales, or persons, living or dead, is purely coincidental.

All rights reserved. No part of this book may be reproduced or transmitted in any form or by any means, electronic or mechanical, including photocopying, recording, or by any information storage and retrieval system, without the author's permission.

1

New York, 1932—

Virginia 'Ginny' Weltermint waved goodbye to her mother and younger brother at the train station in New York and showed her first-class ticket to the blue-uniformed man to board the luxury passenger train *The Sunshine Express* for the five-day return trip to Hollywood. A porter dressed in red, with a gold hat, came to collect her luggage to take to her cabin. She had her pet Siamese cat Scarlet with her on a leash.

The past few months had been difficult for her after Paul, her Hollywood choreographer fiancé of a year, had left her at the altar. By the time she returned to Hollywood, she hoped that almost everyone would have forgotten about the incident. Since she was from a well-known New York theatre family, it had been a scandal and in the newspapers at the time. The fact that Paul had been a few years younger than Ginny, and Ginny herself wasn't exactly a girl anymore, had made it even more scandalous. Ginny had sought refuge with her family at their townhouse in New York for a few weeks after. Now she was on her way to return to her place as one of the most coveted screenwriters of Westerns in Hollywood under her pseudonym Jake Byrne, who kept a low profile and was a mysterious presence in the Hollywood gossip columns, talked about but never seen. Ginny had learned all about cowboys from her uncle, Robert, who'd worked on a ranch in the West, and grew to love the genre.

Often it seemed her brain worked differently than others like her, and she had the ability to become so intensely focused on whatever project she was working on at the time. Everything else faded away. Of course, nobody in the press knew of her Jake identity. The only people who knew were her family, the studio boss she worked with, and some friends.

Following the porter, Ginny turned around one last time before making the ascent with Scarlet leading the way aboard the sleek train.

"Goodbye, mother! Goodbye, Lawrence!"

Both of them smiled wistfully and waved. They had promised to stay until the train departed.

A man of impressive stature and physique bumped into her as soon as she entered the train. She dropped her purse to the ground.

"Pardon me, miss," the man said in an accent that she thought sounded Dutch. He picked up her purse and handed it to her as Scarlet sat at her side.

He tipped his hat to her, and she could see his face clearly for the first time. He was handsome and looked a bit younger than she.

"Thank you," she said, smiling up at him politely.

He offered her his hand to shake. "Hendrik Bergen."

Yes, he was Dutch. She shook his hand and introduced herself.

"Perhaps we could have a drink after you get settled?" he offered. "I'm travelling for business. And you?"

"Returning home from a sort of vacation."

"Sounds intriguing. You'll have to tell me more. How about that drink?"

"Yes, a drink sounds nice, but later. I have to go to my room first and unpack."

"Of course. Before dinner? Say an hour?"

"All right, I'll see you then."

He bowed to her as she walked away, which she found charming, but after what happened with Paul, she'd made a promise to herself to avoid men. For a little while longer, at least, because there had been others before Paul and she knew there would be others after him.

She'd lost track of the porter after bumping into Hendrik, and the man had continued on with her luggage without her. Her ticket said *nineteen,* and she reasoned she had a good enough sense of direction to find her cabin on her own. Another porter was standing nearby and pointed the way out to her. She caught up with the first porter, and he didn't seem to comprehend that she hadn't been behind him the entire time. She planned to tip him well regardless, as her father, who had passed on last year, leaving his estate to his family, had stressed the importance of tipping throughout her childhood.

Ginny now walked ahead of the porter toward the sleeping car and into her private cabin, which was as spacious and as lovely as the brochure had suggested. Behind the curtained window, she would have a marvelous view of the passing scenery once the train left the station.

The porter set down her luggage, and she thanked and tipped the man. He set her key on the table and shut the small door behind him. Ginny began to unpack her belongings but soon grew tired and left it for later. She checked her watch. She had plenty of time to explore the train before meeting Hendrik for that drink. She heard the conductor announcing the train's departure soon.

She set out to the smoking car, where she would have a good view of the station outside. She planned to wave goodbye to her family. The late spring afternoon weather outside was warm, but inside the train, she was cool in her dress and jacket. Soon it would be evening-time. Her heels clacked on the surface as she went inside the smoking car with Scarlet in tow.

She sat next to an ebullient, plump older couple and lit a cigarette. Even seated, the woman seemed short and stout, and her bewhiskered husband looked as round and nearly as short as she.

They introduced themselves to her as the Warwicks.

Mr. Warwick looked down at Scarlet seated at Ginny's feet and exclaimed, "I don't think I've ever seen a cat on a leash!"

"Her name's Scarlet," Ginny said and introduced herself.

"You're the daughter of the New York Weltermint acting duo, aren't you?" Mr. Warwick asked. He seemed fascinated by the possibility.

Ginny nodded. She didn't dare tell them about her screenwriting career, because she had to be careful.

Like with everyone else, she let them assume she was simply a rich woman.

Mrs. Warwick seemed a touch bothered by the confirmation, and Ginny thought that perhaps she didn't approve of entertainment people. But she gradually became more cordial.

"Traveling by yourself?" Mrs. Warwick asked Ginny. She seemed to be searching Ginny's finger for a ring.

Ginny nodded slowly. She didn't know how they'd react, being of the older generation. Some people of their age still thought it improper for a single woman to be traveling across the country without an escort. The women of Ginny's family had always considered themselves to be independent, starting with her grandmother, who had also been an actress.

"I'm going to Hollywood," Ginny said.

"How interesting," Mr. Warwick said. "It must be exciting being from such a talented family."

Ginny noticed they didn't ask her whether she had a career, and she would have had to answer no if they'd had. They seemed to assume that her going to Hollywood just made sense because of her family.

Mrs. Warwick patted her hand. "You must be careful. There are many men about here looking to deceive a nice-looking, unaccompanied lady such as yourself."

Ginny thought of Hendrik and almost chuckled. She put out her cigarette in the ashtray on the little table in front of them.

"Don't worry, my dear," Mr. Warwick said to his wife. "We'll keep an eye on her." He gave Ginny a look that perhaps a grandfather or uncle would have given her. "We're headed to California as well, to visit our son and his family, but they don't live in Hollywood," he told her.

Ginny didn't need anyone 'keeping an eye' on her, but to protest would look uncouth, so she merely thanked the couple and turned her attention to the people waving goodbye on the train platform. The whistle sounded, and the train lurched forward, and Ginny could feel the motion of the wheels as they left the station. Ginny joined in with everyone else and waved goodbye to the people outside. Her mother and brother appeared to have left already. So they hadn't waited after all. Lawrence would be on his way back to university to finish the term and their mother returning home to the family's townhouse across the street from the grand museum. Her family had been fortunate that the Depression hadn't cut much into their wealth.

Ginny thought of Paul and how he would be sitting next to her if it hadn't been for his cold feet, assuming they even returned to New York at all. They were supposed to have gone to Europe after their wedding. But now Paul was set to marry Ginny's younger, former friend, the singer, Beth Bright, which had inflamed the scandal further. In Hollywood and the gossip columns, Ginny had been known as Paul Blair's "girl" and the daughter of a New York theatre dynasty. But both Paul and Beth knew of her screenwriting identity. Both had kept it a secret, which Ginny felt would continue. Apparently, Beth and Paul had been carrying on for quite some time behind Ginny's back. She was the reason for Paul's cold feet. Ginny had sold the bungalow she'd lived in with Paul and taken a small apartment.

Beth had tried to reach out to her through Ginny's mother, who she knew through the theatre. Ginny hadn't replied. Although enough time had passed that she no longer despised Beth and Paul, she still didn't like either of them. Ginny reasoned she wouldn't protest their engagement, which she had read about in the newspaper, but she wouldn't congratulate them either. That had been part of Ginny's reason for leaving California a few weeks ago, since she hadn't wanted to be around for the aftermath in the press. The announcement in the newspaper had said that the couple would be getting married in Beverly Hills in the summer and were looking forward to starting a family after their marriage. Paul had told Ginny he didn't want to have children.

She looked around the car, which had filled up with many passengers, to see if she could spot Hendrik. But there were too many people seated or walking about for her to really look. She checked her watch as the train rode farther and farther away from the station. Soon the platform seemed small in the distance. She needed to meet Hendrik in a few minutes before the evening meal was served in the dining car. She said goodbye to the Warwicks and half-expected them to follow her. They didn't, but she sensed their eyes on her as she left. Ginny carried Scarlet as she walked.

Inside the red-and-white lounge car, she checked in with the man at the front, who said she could bring Scarlet inside the lounge but not into the dining car, and found Hendrik seated at a corner table, smoking a cigarette. He had waited to order a drink until she arrived. Ginny set Scarlet on the ground and walked her on the leash. Hendrik stood up as Ginny approached his table and waited for her to sit before sitting down again himself, like a true gentleman.

Hendrik smiled attractively across at her. She could see his face very well in the lounge with its wide windows looking out to the passing grey urban scenery, and it was a very nice face. Soon the lounge would be lit for the nighttime.

"I'm glad you could join me," he said.

"And I as well," Ginny said.

A waiter appeared, and they ordered lemonade, given Prohibition.

"Are you alone on the journey?" he said. "I realize I should have inquired about that before asking you to join me." He seemed to be searching her hand for a ring, just like Mrs. Warwick had. From the look in his eyes, she felt he wouldn't have minded if she had been wearing a ring and that he would have been just as comfortable continuing as they were.

"Yes," Ginny said. "I'm not with anyone."

"In that case, would you like to join me for dinner?" He sounded pleased.

Ginny couldn't deny his appeal, but it was too soon after Paul for her to be interested in romance, and she sensed Hendrik was. She didn't want to spend her night attached to a man, or the entire trip back to California for that matter. "Not tonight. Maybe tomorrow. Lunch, perhaps?" Lunch seemed less intimate than dinner.

His gaze clouded over with disappointment. He said with a grin, "Looks like I will have to wait. We'll have lunch tomorrow."

The waiter brought their drinks to the table. Ginny took a cigarette out of her bag, and Hendrik lit it for her.

Hendrik gestured at Scarlet by Ginny's feet. "Say, it's quite funny you keep your cat on a leash."

"She wouldn't have it any other way."

Hendrik smiled at Scarlet genuinely and reached down to stroke her, and she hissed at him.

Ginny laughed. "I don't think she likes you very much."

"No, she doesn't," he said with a laugh.

"What kind of business are you in, Mr. Bergen?" Ginny asked him.

"I work for an automotive company," he said.

Ginny felt that his answer was a bit evasive. "And what do you do there?" she asked.

"I'm an engineer."

"How intriguing." Ginny wished she knew something about engineering so she could ask him a thoughtful question or two. But her parents had both been acclaimed stage actors and theatre owners, now retired—their marriage had been somewhat of a scandal at the time given that her mother had gotten divorced from her first husband so she could marry Ginny's father—and Lawrence, the odd duck out in the family, was studying medicine at university and not going in to a career in the arts. Ginny herself had gone to college to study Literature and the Classics and had taken courses in writing.

"What brings you to California?" Ginny asked. "You mentioned business, so I assume you aren't traveling for leisure or returning home."

"The company I work with, Blue Automobiles in New York, where I live, wants to expand out in California. I'm assuming a woman like you owns a Blue."

"Don't so many these days?" Ginny said. A Blue

auto was almost as popular among her crowd as a Rolls Royce.

"Yes, of a certain income. I don't own one myself. I must admit I am a bit of a communist," he joked.

Ginny laughed. "Don't tell me you still use a horse and carriage?" She gave him a wink.

Hendrik smiled from ear-to-ear. "I have to say I find you very intriguing, Miss Weltermint. It's not often that a young lady of your standing—you are related to the Weltermint theatre empire, aren't you—travels by herself."

Ginny was flattered he'd referred to her as a "young lady" when she wasn't exactly young anymore.

"Yes, Joseph Weltermint was my father."

"I was sorry to read of his death in the newspaper."

Ginny thanked him. After a moment, she gave him her reason for her New York vacation, and she vaguely told him about Paul. Hendrik acted surprised when Ginny had thought he would have heard of the incident in the papers. "You really didn't know?" she said.

"Not in the least."

"The Warwicks said a similar thing to what you said—about my traveling alone."

"Who are they?"

"An older couple I met in the smoking car."

"They don't approve of single ladies traveling alone?"

"No, they don't seem to."

"Why not?"

"I believe it's because of men like you."

"Men like me?"

"Yes, men who ask women they don't know to join them alone for drinks."

"The lounge isn't my cabin," he countered.

"True," Ginny said with a grin. "I certainly wouldn't have gone with you alone in there."

Hendrik laughed, and Ginny did as well. Her boldness was one of the things that Paul had said he'd cherished most about her. Then he'd gone and left her for Beth.

"Do you travel to California often for business?" Ginny asked Hendrik.

"Sometimes. I prefer the train to driving, which takes longer. I don't like boats either because I can't swim, which is a problem when I have to travel to Europe for business, which is once in a while. Have you ever been to Europe? I'm assuming a lady of your class would have been there more than once."

Ginny thought of the trip she had been supposed to take with Paul, then she nodded. She didn't want to discuss Europe at the moment.

"You're the opposite of me, I love the water," she said. "I was a competitive swimmer at the women's college. Of course, at the time, a few people thought it scandalous that I appeared in public in a bathing suit."

"I bet you looked gorgeous in your bathing suit." He grinned.

Ginny nearly dropped her cigarette at his brazenness, but she didn't want him to see the effect he had on her, so she stabilized herself. Scarlet purred against her legs under the table, calming her.

"I'll have to teach you to swim someday," she said in a matter-of-fact tone.

"I'd certainly like that, when the weather is a bit warmer. And what do you do; do you work?"

Many assumed that because of her family's status she wouldn't need to work, and she didn't reveal her

Jake Byrne identity to just anyone. She had to trust them first. It would create quite a scandal if the press got wind that Jake was actually a woman and that he was Ginny Weltermint, no less. At first, no one in Hollywood had even known her true identity. She had submitted her scripts to the studios under her alias, and once she secured interest from them, a few hadn't wanted to work with her after learning of her true identity. But the biggest name in Hollywood, the studio boss Mickey Goldstein of Gilded Pictures, had taken a chance on her, and she still worked for him today. Could she trust Hendrik with her secret? The newspapers would go wild over a female Western screenwriter. But for some reason, she felt she could trust Hendrik, though she'd only just met him, so she told him about Jake. He didn't live in California, and she'd probably never see him again outside the train anyway.

"How fascinating. I have heard of Jake Byrne." He didn't seem shocked but intrigued.

"It doesn't shock you?" she asked.

"Not at all. I admire you, actually."

She found his take on it modern and refreshing.

"Do you have someone else to have dinner with tonight?" he asked.

"I imagine they'll sit me with some interesting people." Ginny wondered if he would push the dinner invitation on her again. But they finished their drinks and parted ways before they could order another. Hendrik kissed her hand.

"I will see you tomorrow at lunch," he said.

Charming, Ginny thought, but too obvious to pursue. She could only imagine the further sensationalist articles that would ensue in the newspapers if she brought home a lively Dutchman so soon after the disaster at the altar. Her mother was understanding, but that might be a breaking point for the public. Then again, Paul had seemingly been so stable yet left her in the end. Perhaps what she needed was a bit of excitement this time around.

Ginny walked to her cabin to get ready for dinner. She thought she felt someone watching her and checked behind her to see if the Warwicks were there, but there was just a group of children scampering about as their glamorous mothers in hats stood near them, observing. She thought nothing more of it and went inside her cabin. She glanced out at the now dark sky, closed the curtains and let Scarlet sit on the bed.

Ginny unpacked her typewriter and record player and played some jazz music as she prepared for the evening. Scarlet rolled and purred along to the beat of the music. Ginny dressed in a blue and white dress with a strand of shiny, dark pearls and black shoes. She turned off the music when a song came on – the female singer reminded her of Beth.

Ginny looked at herself in the mirror in her room. She cut a stylish figure with her rounded hips, and with her ginger hair swept up in a twist, making her brown eyes seem dramatic. She put on more red lipstick and added a little rouge and a spritz of perfume. She selected a beaded purse from her luggage and was ready for the night.

Ginny said goodbye to Scarlet on the bed—she trusted her enough not to put her in a carrier—and left her room clutching her purse. She hoped that she really would be seated with some interesting people at dinner. Hendrik probably had thought he could bribe a waiter so they could have sat together. Ginny smiled to herself and, for a moment, regretted turning him down. He would have certainly made interesting company. She would stop and chat with him at dinner if she ran into him, and if she didn't, they would have lunch together tomorrow.

Outside her cabin, the Warwicks were walking toward her.

"Leaving dinner early?" Ginny asked them. But as far as she knew, dinner hadn't even been served yet.

"Mrs. Warwick feels queasy," Mr. Warwick explained.

"I'm very sorry to hear that," Ginny replied.

Mrs. Warwick did look pale.

"We were on our way to eat, and then she felt terrible. It's unfortunate because I heard they're supposed to serve a lovely meal," Mr. Warwick said. "I'm afraid you'll have to do without our company."

Ginny would never say it aloud, but she was a little relieved they wouldn't be keeping an eye on her in the dining car. She could only imagine what they'd think of her if they knew she had a career and what it was. She gave them a polite smile and went on her way. The Warwicks went into their room behind her and shut the door.

An attractive young blonde woman, a girl, really, in a rather plain dress, crashed into her. Her perfume smelled of lilac.

"Oh, I'm terribly sorry," Ginny said.

In silence, the woman didn't look at her and continued walking quickly, running almost. Why was she in such a hurry?

For a moment, Ginny wondered what the woman was up to, for her behavior was so peculiar. She went on her way and walked past a room with the door opened. She saw a man lying on the floor in the room, which was strange in itself, as was the fact that he wasn't moving. Ginny stopped on her heels, turned around, and walked back to the room. What she saw made her gasp.

The man was in a tuxedo, as though he'd dressed for dinner, and he appeared to be dead.

2

THE TRAIN HAD STOPPED IN A SMALL VILLAGE OUTSIDE New York City, and the conductor himself went around making an announcement that everyone was ordered to stay aboard and in their places for the time being. This led to some grumbling by the passengers. Ginny had gone and obtained a member of the train crew after discovering the body. Then she had been asked by the crewman to wait for the lawmen outside the cabin since she was now a witness. The man looked surprised that she seemed unfazed, but inside, she was nervous, and she had to sit down for a few moments in an empty cabin to gather herself after making the grisly discovery.

"Dare I say how inconvenient this is?" a gentleman in a tan suit spoke to his brunette acquaintance as they passed by Ginny on their way to their cabin.

"Apparently someone has died, Thomas. What did you expect?" the woman replied.

A detective and his team were arriving to investigate, the conductor had assured everyone. Some of the crew had covered the deceased with a tablecloth in the name of decency, and they stood guard in front of the door so that no one could enter.

Still in her evening clothes, Ginny leaned against the wall clutching her purse and waited for the lawmen. A small, older man in a suit with a scowling expression approached her, trailed by two policemen in uniforms. He stopped by Ginny, peeked into the cabin with the covered body, and introduced himself as "Detective Keating" without bothering to introduce her to the two policemen at his side. He dismissed the crewmen and spoke with Ginny while the two policemen went inside the room and uncovered the body.

While many would have turned away from the sight of the body, Ginny had looked closely at the man before the crew draped him and noticed that he appeared to have been stabbed. She'd had an interest in detective work ever since she was a girl, an interest which had amused her parents, but bothered others she told, who thought the idea of a woman being interested in law work was uncouth. The interest intensified once she'd started writing. Many of her Westerns had a mystery aspect to them.

The Warwicks had gone into their room and shut the door by the time Ginny came across the man. Ginny told the detective about the young woman she'd seen fleeing the area where the body was found.

"Yes, yes," he said, writing down the description Ginny gave of the woman. "Do you know this woman, or perhaps you recognize her from around the train?" he asked.

"No, but we only boarded this morning."

"And your full name is?"

She gave it to him.

"Your father is Joseph Weltermint, the theatre actor, isn't he?" Detective Keating asked.

Ginny nodded, but the detective continued, "I never cared for the arts myself. My father was a coal miner back in Pennsylvania, where I plan to return to someday."

She imagined the detective was approaching the age for retirement. "Oh, I see," Ginny said quietly. "I've always had an interest in detective work. As a girl, I wanted to be a detective."

She thought her words would have amused the detective, but he grimaced at her as though tasting something disagreeable.

"You, a lady?" He chuckled at her assertion.

She considered replying, "Why not?" or "How hard could it be?" with a bit of cheek, but she wanted him to tolerate her so that she could hover in the background and participate in the goings-on. "Perhaps," she said coyly instead.

"I am very experienced, miss. In fact, I am nearing retirement, and I can assure you that a woman won't ever make a good detective. There are reasons we have certain rules in place. She might make a policewoman, but being a detective takes a certain composure that women lack."

"Thank you for your insight," she replied with a tolerant smile.

"And where is your room, Miss Weltermint?" Detective Keating asked with an eyebrow raised, as though she might have been visiting a gentleman friend in the vicinity last night when she came across the body.

"I was on my way to dinner. Alone," Ginny said firmly, not enjoying him making an implication about the type of woman she might be. "My room is over there." She gestured to her cabin door. Then she thought of something. Scarlet. Ginny had been waiting for hours, which had been a bore but was getting more exciting now, and she hadn't fed Scarlet her evening meal. "My cat," she said.

Detective Keating raised his eyebrow again.

"She's with me onboard the train. I need to feed her."

"Very well. When we are all finished here, then you can feed your cat." From his tone, he didn't seem to sense her need.

She hesitated, and he said, "Surely that can wait a little longer? A man has died. This is of utmost importance."

"Yes, yes, of course."

He was right, of course, and Scarlet had already waited so long that a few more moments wouldn't matter. Ginny knew that if she wanted to be part of the excitement of the investigation, at least from the outside, she would have to fully immerse herself. She liked that he needed her; it made her feel like a genuine part of the investigation. The situation could make good fodder for her writing, for she had an interest in working on a detective picture.

"And you are the only witness?" Detective Keating cleared his throat, and it made a most unpleasant sound.

"Yes, I was alone when I came across the body," Ginny answered.

"Are you an acquaintance of this man? Do you know his name?"

"I have no idea who he is. I've never seen him before now."

"Not even around the train?"

Ginny shook her head. "But we haven't been on for very long."

"And you were alone at the time of your discovery?"

"Yes, as I said."

"Surely a woman of your..." he said, appearing to be searching for the precise words, "...style," he finished with another clearing of this throat, "would have had some company?" He seemed to be implying, mustn't she have had a gentleman with her at the time?

"No, detective, I can assure you that I was alone. The only other person here at the time was the young woman I told you about. The Warwicks had already gone into their room, behind me." Ginny pointed out their room to the man.

"The Warwicks, and they are? I would like to speak with them."

Ginny explained about the couple, and as if on cue, Mr. Warwick poked his whiskered face out of their room and squinted at them. He appeared to be in his dressing gown and seemed utterly oblivious about what had transpired.

"Say, what is this commotion all about?" Mr. Warwick put on his eyeglasses and stared at Ginny and the detective. Ginny wasn't wearing her watch, but she assumed it would be approaching morning soon, and she wondered about Hendrik and if he'd heard the news about the discovery of the body.

"Someone's been murdered," Ginny told him.

Mr. Warwick's face turned as pale as his wife's had looked when Ginny saw them last.

"We haven't determined the cause of death yet," Detective Keating interjected.

"The man had to have been murdered," Ginny said. "It looked to me like someone stabbed him in the heart. Perhaps whoever did it wanted to show he'd hurt them."

"Now, now, we mustn't discuss this so openly," Detective Keating whispered to Ginny, as though even Mr. Warwick himself could be a suspect.

Was the detective on to something? After all, the Warwicks had been in the vicinity when she discovered the body, but Ginny doubted they could have committed the crime and left in such a short amount of time given their age. Still, she had to wonder. Perhaps Detective Keating had a point. Ginny wanted the detective to speak with Mr. Warwick near her so that she could eavesdrop. She gestured for Mr. Warwick to step over, and Detective Keating eyed her as though she was acting out of turn but still spoke with the man, although aside.

"Please wait here, Miss Weltermint," the detective told Ginny.

Ginny pretended she was rummaging through her purse as Mr. Warwick talked with Detective Keating.

"Was the door open, and did you see the body when you walked past the room?" he asked Mr. Warwick.

"My wife and I hadn't even made it to the dining car yesterday evening before she felt ill and we retreated to our cabin. I didn't notice that a door was opened, but I wasn't looking."

"Did you see a young blonde woman in the area? Perhaps leaving one of the cabins?"

"I don't believe so." Mr. Warwick adjusted his

glasses and looked closely at the detective. "My wife and I saw Miss Weltermint, and we might have seen another woman also, but she didn't have blonde hair."

Ginny remembered that Mr. Warwick hadn't been wearing his eyeglasses when she saw his wife and him, and she interjected, "You weren't wearing your eyeglasses at the time like you are now, Mr. Warwick." Until then, Ginny hadn't seen him with his eyeglasses and hadn't known he needed them.

Detective Keating cleared his throat and seemed irritated she'd interrupted the flow of his questions.

"You're quite right, dear," Mr. Warwick spoke to her.

"So, the blonde woman, perhaps she was there, and you didn't see her," Ginny said to him.

"Or perhaps you were mistaken about what you saw," the detective interrupted Ginny and stared at her.

"No," Ginny said firmly. "I saw a young woman, she had blonde hair, walking quickly out of the vicinity. I'm sure of that."

"Sometimes ladies can imagine things, especially if they want to be detectives," Keating replied.

Ginny disliked his suggestion that she might be a hysterical, lying woman. "I give you my word that it wasn't my imagination."

Mr. Warwick eyed the detective resolutely. "Sir," he spoke. "Are you aware who this kind lady is? Surely a woman of her standing is not easily mistaken."

"I am aware who she is," Keating said to him. "I am also aware that she gave me a very vague description of a mysterious woman who she claims to have seen but you did not. There are over one hundred passengers aboard this train. I can't just order everyone to step outside because she gives me her word. Do you know how many blonde women must be on this train? If she is telling the truth, which you insist she is, how am I supposed to find the correct one?"

Mr. Warwick frowned at the detective. "Pardon me, but you, sir, are a most disagreeable man."

Keating grumbled to himself.

Ginny intruded on their quarrel and emphasized to the detective about the woman's young age and simple dress and lilac perfume.

"She might not be a first-class passenger," Mr. Warwick offered to Detective Keating.

"Either that or she stole the dress," he replied.

Ginny understood that the detective had to look at everything from all angles, but his surliness and old-fashioned views on the female sex weren't in the least bit charming to her. Given the fact that he seemed to be impolite even to a kind, older gentleman like Mr. Warwick led Ginny to conclude that Mr. Warwick's observation of Detective Keating was accurate.

"I can come with you to find the woman," Ginny offered to the detective.

Detective Keating muttered something she didn't catch and then said, "Perhaps."

He continued to speak with Mr. Warwick aside and seemed determined to leave Ginny out of it.

Mrs. Warwick came out of the room in her dressing gown to see what was going on.

"Where has my husband disappeared to?" she asked Ginny.

Before Ginny could explain, Mrs. Warwick saw Mr. Warwick's presence just inside the doorway of the cabin, speaking with Detective Keating, and she went over to them. She shrieked at the sight of the body and collapsed into her husband's arms, who embraced her.

"What are you doing out of bed, dear? You still aren't feeling well," he reminded her.

Ginny thought the woman still looked quite pale.

"Oh, Maurice!" Mrs. Warwick cried. "How shall I ever get the sight out of my mind?"

Mr. Warwick scolded the detective about the body being uncovered, and the detective replied rather curtly, "Forgive me, but we are in the middle of an investigation. We will clear it away as soon as we are able to, sir."

Mrs. Warwick straightened from her husband's shoulder and looked at Ginny. "How ever can you stand the sight of it, my dear? I do hope you are not involved." She gasped.

Mr. Warwick patted his wife's arm. "No, according to the detective here, the lady merely came across it."

"It must have given you quite a fright," Mrs. Warwick said, drying her eyes with the sleeve of her dressing gown. "I wish I had a tissue to offer you." She seemed to be searching Ginny's eyes for tears and looked concerned when she didn't find any.

"Yes, it was quite troubling," Ginny offered, concealing her excitement for the investigation. Yet when she did think of the poor soul who'd died, it bothered her vastly.

Detective Keating spoke to the two policemen in the room. "Both of you, go talk to any blonde women aboard this train to see if they know something."

The two policemen left the man's room to search for the blonde woman Ginny had seen, and Detective Keating now spoke with both of the Warwicks outside the room, with their backs turned to the doorway.

Ginny noticed something with a white edge sticking out of the dead man's suit pocket, and she sneaked past the three into the room and put on her evening gloves. She carefully pulled the white card out of the man's pocket and read the name written in gold cursive. *Little Joe's*. It seemed to be the name of a business, some kind of restaurant or nightclub, perhaps? There was a New York address handwritten on the back of the card, a place she had never been to. Ginny memorized the name and address and returned the card to the man's pocket. She quietly left the room, removed her gloves, and went to her place in the corridor.

Ginny interrupted Detective Keating's conversation with the Warwicks. "May I go feed my cat?"

Detective Keating gave her a look that could have frozen water.

Ginny shrugged, gave him a wide-eyed stare, and continued to lean against the wall. Oh, well, she had to try. Scarlet would be all right for a while longer. She listened as the detective spoke with the Warwicks.

Detective Keating's loud voice rang out in the corridor. "And neither you nor your husband saw this blonde woman Miss Welterment claims to have seen?"

"That's correct," Mr. Warwick replied.

"And what about you, Mrs. Warwick?" Keating asked.

"I'm afraid I don't remember. I was feeling dreadfully ill at the time and had my head down. My husband would remember better."

"Your husband has told me he doesn't believe he saw her. Mrs. Warwick, it would be very helpful if you could remember anything, anything at all," Detective Keating said.

"There might have been a woman walking around—no, I'm not sure. There might have been a woman. I'm not sure."

"Besides Miss Weltermint?" Keating asked.

"Yes. But I don't remember what she looked like and if her hair was blonde. I'm not sure. We went in our room right after running into Miss Weltermint, and she would know better than us."

The detective glanced at Ginny. "Did you see Miss Weltermint entering or leaving the cabin of the deceased?" he asked Mrs. Warwick quietly.

Ginny interjected, "Am I a suspect? I only came across the body. I can assure you I wasn't involved."

"Please be quiet, Miss Weltermint. No one can confirm this mysterious blonde woman yet, and it was you who was in the area of the body. So it is quite possible you are making up this blonde woman and it was you, yourself, who was involved in this man's death."

"I only found him!" Ginny stepped in front of the detective and exclaimed. "I have no connection to this man."

"Or so you claim," Keating stated.

"I was on my way to dinner when I ran into this blonde woman and then saw the man in the room. She might have been involved, but I can assure you, I was not."

"Or you are being untruthful."

"I'm not lying," Ginny said with determination.

Mr. Warwick, who had been listening in to their conversation intently with his wife, intervened once more. "Pardon me, detective, but do you know who this woman's family is? Surely, she is noble and telling the truth."

"A noteworthy family does not make an honest

woman," Keating said, eyeing Ginny with distrust. "As an officer of the law, I must treat everyone equally. Anyone onboard could be the culprit."

He seemed suspicious of her merely *because* of who her family was, not based on any solid facts.

Mrs. Warwick gasped and put her hand to her chest. "Heavens, you don't think we could have done it?"

"On this train, anything is possible, Mrs. Warwick," Detective Keating replied.

Mr. Warwick scowled at the detective. "I don't very much like your assertion."

Mrs. Warwick started sobbing, and Mr. Warwick comforted his wife.

Ginny patted the woman's shoulder. "Perhaps someone jumped off the train after they committed the killing," she suggested to the detective. Given her occupation, her imagination often ran wild, but one could never be sure.

Keating looked at her and raised an eyebrow. "Ridiculous! Do you know how fast an express train like this moves? Whoever killed this man is still on board, I'm certain of that."

3

By then, Detective Keating had asked the train crew to block off the corridor so that no one else could pass during his investigation, but Hendrik appeared.

Hendrik approached the group in the corridor and whispered to Ginny, "I managed to sneak past the crew to see what was happening. I heard a body had been found but didn't know you were involved. Are you all right?" He looked from her to the Warwicks.

Ginny nodded. "I only came across it."

Hendrik offered a sympathetic pat on her shoulder.

"Sir, what are you doing here?" Detective Keating said to Hendrik. "You're not supposed to be here."

Hendrik handed Keating what looked like a business card. "Are you the detective who's investigating? Hendrik Bergen." He offered his hand.

The detective stared at Hendrik's hand as he shook it. "Yes, sir, I am. Detective Keating." He read the card Hendrik had given him. "Your business card is impressive, Mr. Bergen, but it does not answer my question as to why you are here. You must have somehow gotten past the guards. Perhaps you have something to add to the investigation? You're an acquaintance of Miss Weltermint's?"

"I am, detective."

"Were you with her at the time she claims to have seen this mysterious blonde woman?" Keating asked Hendrik.

Hendrik seemed to be looking to Ginny for how to answer him, as though he wondered whether he might need to give her an alibi.

"It's okay, Hendrik," Ginny said.

"No," Hendrik spoke to the detective. "We had a drink in the lounge in the afternoon."

"Do you know what Miss Weltermint's whereabouts were afterwards?"

Hendrik looked from Ginny to the detective and seemed nervous. "I'm afraid I don't."

"Hmm," Detective Keating said. He looked at Ginny. "So, you do not have an alibi."

"I was here, I found the body," Ginny said, exasperated. "The Warwicks said they saw me, and the blonde woman I told you about saw me, and I wasn't emerging from that man's cabin."

"Yes, yes, and you saw her."

"She might have had something to do with what happened to that man," Ginny said. "She seemed quite nervous."

Hendrik interjected when he saw what was going on. "I'm certain Miss Weltermint has nothing to do with what happened. She is an honest woman."

Keating grumbled, "That's what everyone keeps saying." He paused. "How well do you know Miss Weltermint?" he asked Hendrik.

"If you're implying what kind of woman I am..." Ginny started to say.

"No, madam, I am doing no such thing. I am merely trying to discern how familiar Mr. Bergen is with your character. Mr. Bergen says you are an honest woman, and I need to assess how he has drawn this conclusion."

Hendrik waited a moment then confessed, "I only met her today."

"Then, as far as you know, her character could be questionable," Detective Keating said.

Hendrik frowned at the man. "Certainly not. Listen, detective, the kind of business I'm in..." He paused. "Well, let's just say I'm a very good judge of character."

"I see. And based on your being in the..." the detective looked at Hendrik's card again "...automotive business, that makes sense," he spoke with a little sarcasm.

Hendrik had been about to say something else but stopped himself. He frowned at the detective. "I can only assure you that I am, indeed, a good judge of character. Take my word for it."

"Yes, sir, and being a detective, I can assure you that I am a good judge of character as well."

"I don't doubt that," Hendrik said, and Ginny thought she noticed a touch of sarcasm in his voice also.

Ginny took the detective's word to mean he would be the final judge as to whether Ginny might be the culprit.

"I know I saw that woman," she said.

"Yes, and if my men return with her, you will be proven right."

Ginny became worried the woman might not be found. She imagined it would take the policemen some time to find the woman, if they found her at all. A thought crossed her mind: what if the woman had hopped off the train?

Detective Keating turned his attention to the Warwicks, and Ginny clutched at Hendrik's arm. "Wait with me."

"I will," he said, patting her hand, seeming to sense her worry.

Keating told the Warwicks he was finished with them for now and they could return to their cabin.

"I hope your investigation won't take too long," Mrs. Warwick spoke to the detective. "We didn't eat last night, and I could use a meal."

"We'll have some of the waiters come around with tea and coffee and sandwiches at some point once things are more settled," the detective told her.

He didn't seem to mind playing concierge for Mrs. Warwick, and Ginny wondered whether he disliked her in particular or just because she was younger.

Once the Warwicks had gone into their room, the detective told Ginny to wait and excused himself to go inside the dead man's cabin. Hendrik stayed with her. Ginny watched as the detective dusted the man's room for fingerprints. Ginny overheard the detective mumbling to himself about "money seems to be missing."

"I hope those policemen come back soon with the woman I saw," Ginny said to Hendrik.

"I'm sure they'll return soon." Hendrik rubbed her shoulder, and Ginny found herself feeling safe in his warmth.

"I still don't understand how I went from being a witness to a suspect."

"I don't like it either," Hendrik said. "That detective is a bit of a loose cannon if you ask me," he whispered.

"I wish the Warwicks had remembered something. Of course, Mr. Warwick wasn't wearing his eyeglasses at the time. I wish someone would believe I saw that woman."

"I believe you," Hendrik said, smiling down at her.

The two policemen returned, and Ginny overheard them telling Keating that none of the blonde women they found knew anything about the body.

"Perhaps one of them is lying to these men," Ginny suggested to the detective inside the room. "Perhaps you could speak with them yourself."

"Do not enter this room any farther, miss," he said to her. "What in heavens name do you expect me to do, line up all the blonde women aboard this train and interrogate them and see if they smell like lilac?"

"Perhaps I could come with you to find the woman," Ginny suggested. "By the way, did you find any interesting fingerprints?"

The detective stared at her like that wasn't any of her business, then slowly shook his head.

"When did the man die?" Ginny asked.

Again, he looked at her like that wasn't her business. "A little bit prior to the discovery of the body. Regardless, such details don't concern you. And nonsense about you coming with me, I don't have time to go on a wild goose chase with you on this train, miss."

"Perhaps someone could make a sketch of what I remember the woman looking like," Ginny said, stepping outside into the corridor again.

"We don't have someone like that back at the station."

"We could see if there are any artists aboard."

The two policemen looked at each other and nodded, as though they liked her idea. Keating frowned at them.

"I could describe what she looks like, and someone could draw her," Ginny suggested again. "She can tell you that I wasn't in the room when she saw me and that I was approaching from the opposite direction."

Speaking to her in the doorway, Detective Keating put his fingertips to his chin and stroked. He seemed to be thinking. "You remember her well enough for someone to draw her?"

Ginny nodded in confidence.

"Very well," Keating said. He turned to the two policemen and pointed at one of them. "Go see if you can find an artist aboard this train."

The man nodded and went on his way.

"Continue to wait here," Detective Keating told Ginny. He returned to the victim's cabin.

Ginny contemplated whether she should tell Hendrik about the card she found in the man's suit pocket. She wondered if the detective had found it by then and what he'd do with the information once he had. *Little Joe's* could be any kind of place and might not mean anything significant. Perhaps the man had merely had lunch there one afternoon and taken a card with him. But she knew a lot of the restaurants and clubs in the New York area and had never heard of the place. Perhaps Hendrik had. Although she felt she could trust Hendrik, after all, he already knew that she was a secret screenwriter, she decided to keep the card private for now. She also decided not to tell Keating about the card either and to let him find it on his own, for her having gone through the man's pockets could cast further suspicion on her. She hoped he would find it, for if he didn't, she would have to admit what she'd done. That thought filled her with apprehension.

"Are you all right, Miss Weltermint?" Hendrik looked at her as though she appeared ill.

"Yes, I'm fine, thanks. Just a touch of nerves is all."

"Given the situation, that's to be expected."

"I do hope that policeman will return soon, and the detective will let me be on my way." She explained about Scarlet's meal.

"I would hope so. You've already been standing here for quite some time. Shall I go ask him?"

"No, that's all right. He's a disagreeable man, so I wouldn't bother."

"He is, isn't he?" Hendrik said with a chuckle.

Ginny laughed. "Needless to say, we won't be having our lunch."

Detective Keating came out of the cabin and looked from her to Hendrik. "What on earth is going on out here? Having a good time while a man has been murdered in the other room?" he scolded.

"You're admitting he was murdered?" Ginny said.

Keating cleared his throat, then nodded curtly. "He was stabbed, but we haven't found the knife."

"In the heart?"

The detective nodded.

"Like I thought," Ginny said. "Do we know his name?"

"We, Miss Weltermint? I know his name, yes."

"What is it?" Ginny asked.

When the detective seemed about to protest, Ginny added, "I don't know his face, but I want to see if I recognize the name."

"William O'Connor. Is it familiar to you?"

Ginny shook her head. "Do you know anything about him?"

"At this time, all we know is his name."

Hendrik apologized to the detective about the earlier humor that had passed between Ginny and himself. "We weren't trying to be unkind. I was just trying to cheer up Miss Weltermint."

"Yes, well, regardless, it is inappropriate at this time," the detective replied. "I am sure you realize that such behavior casts further suspicion upon Miss Weltermint."

"Further suspicion?" Ginny exclaimed. "I've already told you countless times that I had nothing to do with this. I merely came across this poor man."

"Yes, well, we'll see what comes up if my man can find an *artiste* to draw this woman you claim to have seen and who can also vouch that you walked by the room from the other direction and so you couldn't have been involved, assuming you weren't trying to throw us off and simply backtracked your steps."

"With all due respect, sir, that is absurd," Hendrik intervened. "As far as I can see, you have no reason to suspect Miss Weltermint of the crime."

"As far as we've confirmed, she was the only person near the vicinity of the body."

"Except for the blonde woman I told you about," Ginny said.

Keating grumbled and returned to the cabin to speak with the other policeman, who was still working inside.

"Most unpleasant," Hendrik reaffirmed.

Ginny murmured in agreement and glanced into the dead man's cabin. Relief drifted through her when she saw that Detective Keating was finally going through the man's pockets. She was confident he would find the card and make it part of the investigation. Ginny wanted to be involved because she found it interesting, but at the same time, she knew that too much eagerness could look suspicious, as though she wanted to be involved to see how much the investigators knew.

Moments later, the policeman Detective Keating had sent to search the train for someone to draw the woman Ginny had seen returned with a nervous-looking young man. The policeman called for the detective, who stepped out into the corridor. The young man held some kind of pad in his hand.

"You're an artist?" Keating asked him.

The young man nodded with his eyes wide. "I'm a student at the Art Society."

"A painter?"

"Yes."

"Do you have your paints with you?"

"No."

"Doesn't matter anyway. We don't have time for you to compose a painting."

The young man introduced himself as Amos and held up the sketchpad and charcoal he carried in his hand. "I brought my sketchpad and charcoals so that I can draw." He nodded at Hendrik and Ginny.

"I suppose we should consider ourselves lucky that you brought those aboard the train." Detective Keating smiled in a forced way, as though he wasn't exactly pleased that Ginny's idea might work out after all. "Are you any good? You don't draw cartoons or something, do you?"

Amos shook his head. "No, sir. I consider myself to be a classical painter."

"This should be interesting. Very well, Miss Weltermint here will describe to you the woman we wish for you to draw for us." He pointed out Ginny to the boy, as though it wasn't already obvious given that Ginny was the only "Miss" among them. "I would appreciate if you made this quick."

The young man nodded as though he understood the detective's urgency. "Yes, sir. I'll work as fast as I can."

The other policeman came out of the room and joined Detective Keating, and the three lawmen stood around as though they were all going to watch Amos work right there in the corridor.

Amos dropped his sketchpad and charcoal to the floor, and Ginny noticed a sheen of perspiration on the young man's brow.

"Perhaps we could go somewhere quiet where this young man could work with less pressure?" Ginny suggested.

The nervous boy looked at her with gratitude.

"That's a good idea," Hendrik said.

"One of my policemen will have to come with you," Detective Keating groused. "I can't have you running about the place."

"Worried I might sneak off the train?" Ginny said in jest.

"That would be highly unlikely, miss. We have men stationed at all the exits."

Detective Keating ordered one of the policemen to come with Ginny and Amos into an empty cabin nearby.

Ginny sat down across from the young man, who leaned his sketchpad against his knee and held the charcoal mid-air. The policeman stood just outside the door.

"Ready to begin when you are, miss." Amos gave her a shy smile.

Ginny did her best to describe the woman she'd seen, and the young man worked furiously on the drawing. He showed it to her on completion.

"You're very talented," Ginny remarked with a smile. "That looks very much like the woman I saw."

"Thank you for your kind words, miss," Amos said, blushing.

They rose and went to the policeman in the doorway.

"We're all finished," Ginny told him.

She took the sketch from Amos, and the policeman escorted them back to Detective Keating, who waited for them in the corridor with Hendrik and the other policeman.

Keating nodded at Amos as though he wanted the boy to hand him the sketch. Amos pointed at Ginny.

She held out the drawing, and the detective took it from her.

"I'm surprised you haven't left," Ginny told Hendrik as Detective Keating looked over the sketch.

"I wanted to offer you my assistance," Hendrik replied.

Ginny thanked him.

Keating held the drawing up to the light in the corridor. "She's quite a beauty." He started to hand the sketch to one of his men then retreated. "I shall find her myself. We shall see just how truthful you are being, Miss Weltermint, about this mysterious woman."

"Say, that isn't fair," Hendrik told the man. "All

signs point to Miss Weltermint not being involved in any of this."

"Perhaps you should leave the detective work up to the detectives, sir."

Keating ordered the two policemen to take the body away so he could set off in search of the blonde woman. "When you've finished, you can help the train crew maintain order and keep the exits secure in case someone tries to rebel and hop off."

The men nodded and went inside the cabin to cover the body and carry it away on a stretcher that they had brought with them.

4

THE TWO POLICEMEN DISAPPEARED DOWN THE CORRIDOR with the body, which looked rather short, on the stretcher. Detective Keating mumbled about setting off to "Perhaps find this woman." He went down the corridor.

Ginny and Hendrik looked at each other and followed him. He seemed to ignore their presence but glanced over his shoulder at them every so often.

Ginny smiled at the detective, gracious in the face of his frostiness.

"We'll follow him until he grows tired of us," Hendrik said to her with a grin.

Ginny had been isolated from the rest of the train for quite some time and wasn't able to see what had gone on in the meantime. But it looked as though passengers were generally being respectful of the policemen's orders to stay put. Most were staying in the cabins, but a few passengers had ventured out to the sitting areas and were chatting among themselves. There were too many passengers for the police to really keep them in place. An elderly couple eyed her and Hendrik with suspicion as they passed by their seats, as though since they were trailing Detective Keating who projected an air of authority as he strode, they might be part of the crime.

"I say, when will the dining car open?" a portly man complained to the man seated next to him.

Two young boys were cluttering the area as Ginny and Hendrik and the detective attempted to pass.

Keating stopped and spoke to the boys at their level. "Where are your parents?"

He seemed to be making an attempt at cordiality, which surprised Ginny.

One of the boys stuck his tongue out at the detective, and the other boy howled with laughter. Detective Keating straightened himself. His face turned bright red, and he shook his finger at the boys.

"Where are your parents?" he asked again.

Both of the boys stuck their tongues out at the detective and bolted away.

Ginny and Hendrik looked at each other, and Ginny controlled her laughter, but barely.

Keating turned around and glared at her. "I suppose you find such boorish behavior amusing."

Ginny shook her head as she continued to laugh. "Not at all, detective."

Detective Keating eyed Hendrik. "And what about you, sir?"

"I'm in agreement with the lady."

Keating continued to walk slowly and look over the passengers in search of the blonde woman in the sketch. Ginny and Hendrik continued to follow him.

Morning had arrived and, gradually, people were being allowed to move from their cabins, but not too far. Ginny hadn't seen where the train had stopped until then. Outside the windows, the scenery had become lusher and greener. Ginny spotted a few white cottages with colorful window-boxes in the distance. It looked like a small village in farm country.

A group of what looked like college students were seated in a corner reading books. Detective Keating approached a young lady among them whose hair Ginny felt was more ginger than blonde.

"Excuse me, miss?" he said.

Ginny tapped his shoulder. "She's not really blonde, and, besides, she's not the girl I saw."

Keating ignored Ginny. It was as though Detective Keating was determined to find the young woman on his own, using the sketch, despite that Ginny, the witness, was right there with him.

The detective took out his notepad and introduced himself to the girl, who looked confused. "Do you have anything you'd like to share with me?"

She stared at him with her eyes wide and shook her head.

"And what is your name, please, miss?" Keating asked.

"Margot York," the girl said quietly.

He gestured at Ginny behind him with Hendrik. "Do you recognize this woman?" he asked the girl.

Now the girl looked frightened that a policeman was questioning her. By then, the whole train was abuzz with the news that a body had been discovered and that the man had probably been murdered. People eyed one another with mistrust and wondered, who among them could have done it?

She shook her head. "Should I?"

Ginny tapped the stout Keating's shoulder. "She isn't the girl," she whispered.

The detective swatted Ginny's hand away as if it were a fly.

"Perhaps not," Keating told the girl. "Did you perhaps come across something unpleasant in the corridor earlier? Or did you cause it?" He eyed her skeptically.

One of the young men with her, a boy in a necktie, stood up and faced the detective. "Say, what is this?

Keating put his hands to his hips and tried his best to stand tall in front of the boy, who was a lot larger than he. "I am sure you are aware that a crime has been committed aboard this train."

"Yes, we heard about it." He explained that he and his friends were college students from New York on an exciting trip to California before their examinations. "Margot had nothing to do with it."

"Please let the young lady speak for herself," Keating replied.

"Sam's my fellow," Margot said, standing up next to him.

"Yes, well. Once you've answered my questions, we can clear this matter up."

"She knows nothing," Ginny said. "She's not the girl I saw, detective."

"Margot's been with us the entire time," the other girl with them spoke from her seat. "She hasn't been part of anything sinister."

"Even at night?" Keating asked the young people.

"Even at night," the boy answered, his face turning red.

Detective Keating looked shocked at the implication but stayed silent, and Ginny wondered whether he'd continue to badger the poor girl and her friends. He cleared his throat and went on his way. Ginny apologized to the kids, and she and Hendrik hurried after the detective, who glanced over his shoulder every so often to give Ginny and Hendrik a displeased glance.

Keating stopped to speak with a member of the train crew, and so Ginny and Hendrik caught up to him.

"You may hand out coffee and tea and sandwiches to the passengers in a while," the detective said to the crewman. "My men will allow you to move about to do so. The passengers need to stay in the vicinity of where they already are. Of course, they can stand up and so on to use the facilities—we can't order everyone to remain in place indefinitely—but they shouldn't move too far about. Is that understood?"

The man said, "Yes, sir."

From one of the seats, a man grabbed Keating's sleeve, and the detective shook him off. "What in the devil are you doing, sir?"

"You're a detective, aren't you?" the man said. "When is this thing going to be moving again? My wife is expecting me home in a few days."

"Sir, a man has been murdered. I'm afraid that takes priority over your schedule."

The man gave him an annoyed look as the detective continued on his way. Ginny and Hendrik followed after him. Up ahead, there was the back of a blonde woman's head, but Ginny couldn't see the woman's face or even her profile from that distance. Ginny pointed out the woman to Detective Keating.

"Detective, that woman up ahead. I can't see her face clearly, but we should approach her," Ginny said.

He spoke over his shoulder, "I'll decide that, Miss Weltermint."

"Ginny is only trying to be of assistance," Hendrik said.

"I am aware of that, Mr. Bergen." He paused. "I shall approach this woman."

The woman peeked back at them and started to rise from her seat. Detective Keating shouted at her to stop.

"Madam, do not move!"

The woman seated next to the blonde gasped when she saw the detective approaching, as though the blonde woman could be the killer.

The crewman at the end of the aisle had abandoned his post, and the blonde woman made it to the aisle. She stopped in her tracks and turned around to face the detective.

"Where do you think you are going, madam?" Keating asked her when they reached her place. "No one is supposed to be moving about the train at this time."

"I can't sit any longer. It's vastly boring," the woman griped. "I was just going for a walk to see if I could get something to drink."

"In such a hurry?" Ginny couldn't help but ask.

"And who are you?" she asked.

Ginny stepped forward and held out her hand to the woman. "Ginny Weltermint."

The woman gave her a half-smile, and they shook hands. "Priscilla Dover." She didn't look young enough to be the woman Ginny had seen, and she was too tall.

Keating glanced at Ginny and motioned for her to be quiet. "Do you know this woman, Miss Dover?"

"Mrs. Dover," she corrected him.

"She isn't the woman I saw," Ginny told the detective.

"Are you part of the investigation, like a lady PI, or perhaps a criminal?" Mrs. Dover asked Ginny excitedly.

"She is a witness," Detective Keating interrupted.

"Yes, I'm afraid I'm only a witness," Ginny said to the woman.

"Do you have anything you'd like to share with us, Mrs. Dover?" Keating questioned.

"No. I just wanted to go for a quick stroll."

"How about before then, say, about something that happened last night?"

"Are you suggesting I might have something to do with the murder?" Mrs. Dover trilled with excitement. "How exciting! Am I going to be interrogated?"

Detective Keating seemed vexed. "I'm not sure, Mrs. Dover, should I be questioning you?"

"Are you being serious?" Mrs. Dover said with a smirk.

"Oh, I most certainly am, madam."

"In that case, I don't know what on earth you're talking about. My husband, he can confirm my whereabouts for you. He's found a seat somewhere over there." She gestured. "It's a shame we couldn't sit with each other, but it's so crowded. We had dinner last night and after that, were asked to return to our cabin, where we stayed until they let us leave just this morning but not too far. I don't see why it's really needed, but if you insist, he can confirm my whereabouts for you. Oh, Stewart!" She waved at a balding man seated two rows ahead.

The man turned around in his seat at the mention

of his name. He waved at her and gave her a wan smile but remained seated.

"Stand up, Stewart, and come over here," Mrs. Dover said with exasperation at her husband.

Mr. Dover finally rose and trotted over. "I thought we weren't supposed to walk around," he told them when he reached them.

"There are exceptions," Keating answered the man. "Can you confirm your wife's whereabouts yesterday evening?"

"You're a detective." Mr. Dover's mouth hung open. "Is she under suspicion? How is that possible?"

"Aboard this train, it seems anything is possible," Detective Keating replied.

Ginny started to emphasize again how Mrs. Dover wasn't involved, but Keating shushed her.

"Why did you seem to be fleeing when I first approached you?" Detective Keating asked Mrs. Dover.

"I say, this is outrageous. My wife has done nothing of the sort," Mr. Dover said. He looked at his wife. "You don't have to answer that question, dear."

"It's all right, darling," she said, touching his arm. She looked at the detective. "I didn't think anything of it. I just knew I wanted to go for a walk. I didn't know you were a detective until you told me so. Truthfully."

Ginny couldn't tell if Keating believed the woman, although Ginny already knew she wasn't the right woman.

"Very well, and I can see that you two don't recognize each other," Detective Keating finally said to Ginny and Mrs. Dover.

The crewman reappeared, and Detective Keating scolded the man for leaving his place. He turned to face the passengers and reminded them to remain in their places for the time being. Ginny suggested the three split up to see if they could find the woman Ginny had seen. Hendrik studied the sketch for a moment before the detective snatched it away.

"Do not disembark from this train," he said to Ginny and Hendrik over his shoulder.

Ginny was a bit surprised he'd agreed to let her out of his sight for a while.

"Good luck to us," Hendrik said to Ginny before they parted ways in the opposite direction to search for the woman.

Ginny peered behind her and saw Hendrik's back as he walked away toward the smoking car to look for the woman. She strode along the aisle, past rows of seats, to the dining car, where she planned to check for the woman first. She found the tables in the car, with sunlight pouring in through the windows and casting a glow on the white tablecloths, entirely empty of passengers. The only person in the place was a man at the front, a train employee.

"You aren't supposed to be walking about the train," the man approached her and said.

Ginny tried to explain that she had permission from the detective investigating the case, but he just looked at her as though she was making it up.

"Please return to your cabin or one of the seats, miss," the man said. He started to call to another man, another employee, to escort her there, but Ginny made a dash for the lounge car a few feet down the aisle.

5

THE DOOR TO THE LOUNGE CAR WAS SHUT, BUT GINNY managed to get it open. She peered around the darkened car, with the curtains closed, which looked empty until she spotted someone seated at one of the tables toward the back.

"Hello?" Ginny said, pulling back the curtain.

The figure moved, and Ginny now saw that it was a woman, and her hair looked blonde.

Was she hiding from the police inside the car?

The blonde woman started to rise from the table, as though she might try to bolt. Ginny stepped in front of her.

"My name is Ginny Weltermint," she said, immediately recognizing the woman as the one she'd been searching for. "I believe we know each other."

The young woman looked down at the floor then looked up but wouldn't meet Ginny's gaze. "I have no idea what you're talking about. Excuse me, I must be on my way."

She tried to walk past Ginny, but Ginny wouldn't move out of her way.

"I don't know what you're doing," the young

woman said in a huff. "But I don't find it humorous in the least."

"Do you have something you'd like to tell me?" Ginny said. "Perhaps something about a man found dead in the sleeping car?"

The girl's face blanched. "I have no idea what you mean."

"I believe you do know. I saw you fleeing from the area just before I came across the body."

"You aren't a policeman," the girl observed. "Why is it any of your business where I was and why?"

"I'm helping with the investigation," Ginny fibbed.

"A lady? I've never heard of such a thing."

"I have permission from the detective to find you. You must remember me. I remember you."

"All right," the girl said. "I remember seeing you. But I had nothing to do with what happened to that man."

"What's your name?"

"Maureen Vix."

"Why are you traveling to California, Miss Vix?"

"I'm going to be an actress, or at least, I want to be one. My mother gave me some money for the train. I'm not even supposed to be in this area of the train since the lounge is for first-class passengers only. I'm in second class."

"What were you doing in the vicinity of that man's cabin?"

Maureen suddenly looked ashamed. "He'd promised to take me to dinner in first class. I met him at the station."

Mr. O'Connor had been trying to seduce the girl, which made him sound like a bit of a crumb, but Ginny still was curious enough to help solve his death.

"Oh, I see," she said.

"He'd asked me to meet him in his room, and when I went there, I saw that he had died. I panicked and fled."

"Why didn't you just tell the police this? They did come around and speak with you earlier, didn't they?" Ginny asked, thinking of the two policemen Detective Keating had sent around the train previously.

"Yes, two policemen did earlier. I was scared that the murderer, who I didn't see, might have seen me and could come looking for me, and I thought the police might blame me. I was also embarrassed because I'd agreed to meet a stranger in his cabin since he'd promised to take me to dinner. So I came in here to hide after the policemen spoke to me. I have nothing to do with what happened to him. Honestly."

Ginny believed the girl's story but wondered if Detective Keating would once she told him.

"Do you know who killed Mr. O'Connor?" Ginny asked the girl.

She shook her head. "I didn't know him, really. He'd just asked me to dinner. He wasn't very good looking but seemed like an all right fellow. I wanted a nice meal, so I agreed to meet him."

"If I bring you to the detective who is in charge, will you tell him what you told me just now?"

"I don't think I can admit to going to that man's cabin. If it gets into the newspapers, my mother will have a heart attack back at home."

Ginny wanted to assure the girl that wouldn't happen, but she couldn't be certain. She would have to convince the girl that she needed to tell the truth regardless of what might occur after.

"I'm surprised your mother is letting you become an actress," Ginny observed.

"She says she respects the arts, ma'am," the girl replied.

"Miss Vix," Ginny said. "It is vital you tell the police the truth and that you saw me walking toward that man's room and not away from it and that he was already dead, or else they will continue to think you or I could be involved in his death in some way."

The girl gasped. "They think I'm involved?" She seemed to fully process what Ginny had told her and looked at her strangely. "Or that you might be involved? Why do they think you could be involved?"

"Because, at the moment, they're not sure if I'm telling the truth about your existence. They think I could be making you up to cover something up."

"But you weren't coming out of that man's cabin when I saw you, and he was already dead."

"Exactly, and that's why you need to tell them the truth about what happened and what you saw."

"I don't think I can, Ginny, if I may call you that?"

Ginny nodded.

"My mother," the girl said. "She'd just die if she read about me going to a man's room. She's somewhat old-fashioned."

Ginny thought of her own mother and couldn't relate, but she said, "I know the type, Maureen, and I'm certain that your honesty is more important to her than one slight indiscretion."

The girl looked at her and seemed to ponder what she'd said. "You don't know my mother."

"If you won't do it for yourself, Maureen, then please do it for me." Ginny disliked having to resort to

Scripted Murder

begging, but in the situation, she hadn't much of a choice.

The girl sighed. "Oh, all right, when you put it like that." She paused. "I'm sorry if I was rude to you earlier."

"That's all right."

Ginny made sure Maureen stayed by her side as they left the lounge car and went down the aisle to look for Detective Keating. They ran into Hendrik near the conductor's booth.

Ginny introduced him to Maureen Vix and explained some of her story, and the young woman smiled at him coyly when he said with a grin, "The pleasure's all mine."

"Do you know where Detective Keating is?" Ginny asked him.

"I'm afraid I haven't seen him since we parted ways, but he should be around here somewhere." Hendrik looked around for him.

"Is he a nice man, this Detective Keating?" Maureen suddenly asked her.

Ginny didn't want to lie, but she also didn't want to alarm the girl. "I'd say he's a very unique man," she told her, and noticed Hendrik giving her a perplexed look.

The girl nodded at Ginny as though the answer made sense.

Ginny heard the detective's voice somewhere in the vicinity and gestured to Hendrik, who pointed him out ahead of them to the right of the aisle in a private corner of the train, conversing with a concerned passenger.

"Should we be worried about some maniac running about the place?" the tan-suited man asked Detective Keating when Ginny and Hendrik approached with Maureen. "How long are you going to keep us stationary? When will the train start moving again?"

"Until I find the culprit," Keating answered.

"How long might that take?" the man asked with a frown.

"How ever am I supposed to know precisely how long it will take, sir?" Detective Keating spoke with indignation. "It will take as long as it does take."

The man huffed at the detective's assertion.

"Now, if you'll excuse me, sir, I must attend to something else," Keating said, eyeing Ginny standing with Hendrik and Miss Vix.

"Detective Keating, may I present Miss Maureen Vix, the young woman I told you about," Ginny said with pride, unable to resist relishing in the fact that she'd been right all along despite Keating's doubts.

She indicated for Maureen to speak, but the girl stood there in silence.

"Go on, Miss Vix, tell the detective what you told me," Ginny said.

Maureen glanced at Hendrik as if she was embarrassed to tell her story in front of him, and perhaps to the detective also, Ginny thought. But perhaps she would be less hesitant in front of the detective alone. She suggested that she and Hendrik step aside so that the girl and the detective could speak alone. She heard Maureen blurting out to Detective Keating that she was a second-class passenger and that her mother had paid for her to make the trip to Hollywood because it was her dream since she was a child to become an actress.

"Is everything all right?" Hendrik asked Ginny as the girl and detective spoke nearby.

"Yes," Ginny said. "The girl's a bit embarrassed about something that occurred so I thought it best for us to step away..." Ginny paused when she noticed Detective Keating and Maureen had stopped their conversation. Surely, not enough time could have passed for the girl to tell him the entire story.

Ginny intervened with Hendrik staying behind. "Is everything all right?" she asked Detective Keating and Maureen.

"I don't know why you brought this young lady here to speak with me," Detective Keating complained. "She says she knows nothing."

Ginny looked at the girl and gave her an encouraging smile. "Miss Vix, you need to tell the detective what you told me in the lounge a few moments ago."

"I..." The girl's mouth moved, but no words came out.

"Well, Miss Vix?" the detective said.

The girl looked at Ginny with tears in her eyes. "I'm sorry, I can't." She started to walk away.

Ginny hurried after her. "Maureen, you have nothing to be ashamed about. You are a beautiful young woman. It makes perfect sense a gentleman would wish to have dinner with you."

The girl slowed down, then stopped. "Ma'am, if this gets out in the newspapers, my mother might never speak to me again..."

"It won't get out in the newspapers," Ginny spoke with confidence.

"Pardon me, ma'am, but how can you be so sure?"

"Detective Keating is a surly man, yes, but he is not a braggart. I am confident he will not release your name to the papers."

"But what about the other policemen? What if they make me tell what I told him in court?"

"He is in charge of the other policemen, and they do what he says. About court, I doubt it will come to that." Without the girl noticing, Ginny had woven her arm through the girl's, and they were walking back to the detective.

"You're sure, ma'am?"

Ginny nodded.

"How can you be so sure my secret is safe?" the girl asked Ginny.

"Because I know something about secrets," she said with a wink. "I have a secret too." Ginny leaned in and whispered her secret to Maureen.

"Oh, that's fascinating," the girl said. "I've never met a woman with that kind of a career before, or someone in show business."

"Remember, it's a secret," Ginny said, placing her finger against her lips. "So, now we each know a secret about each other."

The girl smiled at her. "You seem like a refined lady, and so I trust you," she said.

"Now, you must tell the detective exactly what you told me."

"I hope he won't judge what kind of woman I am."

"A strong woman doesn't care what anyone thinks of her," Ginny educated the younger woman.

"How did you get to be so wise?" the girl asked her.

Ginny shrugged. "You'll do well," she told Maureen. "I'll stay with you while you tell him."

Hendrik had been conversing with the detective, but he stepped aside when Ginny approached with the girl. Ginny found it charming that he had stuck with her the whole time of the ordeal and, by all means, seemed likely to still do so. Perhaps she'd been wrong about his nature previously, and he wasn't just a passing amusement.

Ginny presented Maureen to Detective Keating. "Miss Vix has something she would like to share with you."

"I hope you haven't coerced this girl," the detective replied.

"She's done no such thing," Maureen spoke with outrage. "Madam Weltermint has been nothing but kind to me."

"Very well. Now, what is it you want to tell me, young lady?" Detective Keating asked the girl.

Maureen hesitated again.

"Go on, Maureen," Ginny encouraged her and nodded at the detective.

"Are you sure he's trustworthy, madam?" she asked Ginny.

Ginny looked at the detective and expected him to answer the question.

"I most certainly am, young lady," Keating told Maureen.

Ginny listened as Maureen told him the exact story she'd told Ginny in the lounge car.

"You can confirm Miss Weltermint wasn't fleeing the man's room?" Detective Keating indicated Ginny and asked the girl.

She nodded. "Yes, sir. When I saw her, she was approaching the room, not fleeing from it, and that was after I'd seen the body. So she couldn't have harmed that man, for he was already dead."

"And what about you?" He eyed the young woman with skepticism, and she seemed to tremble under his scrutiny.

"I didn't hurt him," Maureen said. "I'd swear on the Bible if I had one."

"Miss Weltermint cannot claim your innocence since she saw you fleeing *from* the area of the man's cabin," Detective Keating told the girl. "Do you own a knife, miss?"

Maureen shook her head repeatedly. "No, sir."

"I believe her," Ginny said. "I don't think she had anything to do with what happened."

Detective Keating brushed off her proclamation. "You weren't so certain, earlier, madam."

"I was wrong," Ginny said.

Keating ignored her. "You seem like a good girl, if a little misguided," he told Maureen. "But I can't just take your—or Miss Weltermint's—word for it, even if I wanted to. I'll have to search your bunk to see for myself. What is your cabin number?"

"Thirty-seven," the girl said.

Detective Keating hurried to the sleeping car in the second-class part of the train, and Ginny followed him with Hendrik and Maureen. On the way there a few passengers stopped the detective to inquire whether the train would be moving soon, and each time, Detective Keating brushed them off rather impolitely.

Both the second- and third-class cabins consisted of shared bunks with four occupants per cabin. There were two other girls playing cards on one of the lower beds when the group entered. Ginny spotted Maureen's bottle of lilac perfume on the table.

Detective Keating ordered the girls to clear out of the room. They stared at Maureen for a moment as if to ask what was happening and then left when she didn't speak.

Detective Keating pointed to a collection of suitcases on the floor. "Which one is yours?" he asked Maureen.

Maureen indicated to the one with the blue handle, and Keating picked it up and opened it on the bed the other girls had vacated. He rummaged through it, carefully avoiding what looked like undergarments, and came up empty. With a look of dissatisfaction on his face, he closed the suitcase and set it down on the floor. He pointed at the beds.

"Which bed is yours?" Keating asked the girl.

Maureen gestured to a top bunk. Detective Keating, a rather stocky man, asked for assistance from the taller Hendrik.

"Reach up there, under that mattress and see if you feel anything," the detective said.

Hendrik reached up to the mattress and stuck his hand under it and made a sweeping motion. He suddenly stopped and grabbed onto something, coming back with what looked like a bottle of bathtub gin.

Detective Keating grabbed it from Hendrik and examined it. "What do we have here?" He chuckled to himself and looked at the young woman. "I suppose you'll say this isn't yours."

Maureen looked as though she might sob.

"It's mine," Ginny suddenly said.

"Nonsense," Keating said. "How do you expect me to believe that?"

"It's true. Miss Vix was keeping it for me."

"Miss Weltermint is lying," Hendrik said.

Ginny looked at him in astonishment and mouthed to him from behind the detective, "What are you doing?"

Hendrik gestured it was all right. "It's actually mine."

Detective Keating stared at him in utter exasperation. "Mr. Bergen, I don't appreciate your playing games with me, or you, Miss Weltermint, for that matter." He glanced at Ginny and Maureen. "I'll just have to arrest all of you."

"All three of us? You can't do that, that's ridiculous," Ginny said.

"I most absolutely can, miss. It's the law under Prohibition."

There had been rumblings among certain people in her social circle that Prohibition could be ending soon.

"Surely, there are more urgent matters for you to busy yourself with, like the death of Mr. O'Connor?" Ginny said to the detective.

"Ginny's right," Hendrik spoke up. "It makes no sense for you to trouble yourself with this small matter when there's a murder investigation being carried out."

"I will decide what is trivial and what is not," Detective Keating answered.

Maureen just stood there quietly, with her eyes wide. Ginny thought the girl might start sobbing at any moment and wanted to resolve the matter before it came to that.

"You're a very busy man, detective," Hendrik said. "I greatly respect that. But I can't see how bringing all three of us into jail would be beneficial in the long run. Anyone with access to this room could have put the gin in there, and Miss Weltermint has been a help to your investigation, as has Miss Vix."

"Very well. Would you prefer that I sent someone

else to deal with it? One of my other policemen, perhaps? Or would you like for me to take just you, Mr. Bergen?"

"If that's what it takes for you to leave these two women alone, then, yes, go ahead." Hendrik held out his wrists to the detective.

His resolve to protect her inspired Ginny with the possibility of romance, but she couldn't let him go to jail for her.

"Detective Keating, is there some other way we could resolve this?" she asked.

Keating's face turned red. "I hope you are not suggesting a bribe, Miss Weltermint."

"Absolutely not. I think that Mr. Bergen has made a good point. Anyone could have had access to this room, so anyone could have put that there. How can you be so sure it has something to do with the girls staying here?"

"Perhaps a member of the staff is the culprit, is that what you are suggesting?"

"Perhaps. Regardless, I don't see how taking us into jail helps with investigating Mr. O'Connor's murder."

Her comment seemed to compel Detective Keating to think the matter over and see it more clearly.

"I will dispose of this in the toilet, and throw away the bottle," he said after a while. He gave the group a stern look. "But nothing like this can ever happen again. Is that understood?"

The three nodded.

"I want both of you ladies," he spoke to Ginny and Maureen, "to remain onboard with everyone else. I want you to stay within my sight. As far as I'm concerned, both of you are still under suspicion regarding Mr. O'Connor."

Ginny trusted what Maureen had told her, but evidently Detective Keating still didn't trust either of them.

The conductor came by the cabin, looking for the detective, and Keating stepped out to speak with him.

Ginny tried her best to calm the frightened Maureen.

"I can't believe he thinks I could have murdered that man," Maureen told Ginny and Hendrik.

"He thinks the same of me, if it makes you feel any better," Ginny said.

"I don't know if I'll ever make it to Hollywood," the girl told Ginny with a sigh. "It's been my dream for so long."

"Don't be silly, of course you will. You'll need a friend out there when you arrive." Ginny reached into her purse and found a pencil and piece of paper. She jotted down her apartment address for the girl. "If you ever need anything, here's where I am."

Maureen accepted the paper and thanked Ginny. "How can you be so sure he'll declare us innocent after all?"

"These things do have a way of working themselves out," Ginny spoke with confidence. "How would you like to audition for a studio head once you reach California?" she asked.

"You're jesting?" the girl asked.

When Ginny shook her head, there was a sparkle of admiration in the girl's eyes, as though Ginny were a fairy godmother making all her dreams come true.

"Maureen knows about my writing," Ginny explained to Hendrik. "The man I work for," she told

Maureen. "is always on the lookout for new actresses to feature in his movies. And I'm certain you are probably as talented as you are beautiful."

"Oh, ma'am, I'm ever so grateful." Maureen started to lower herself down, and Ginny wondered whether she'd kneel at her feet. She touched the girl's soft hair. "It's quite all right, dear, you can stand up."

Maureen embraced Ginny, and Hendrik smiled at the two.

Detective Keating returned and told Maureen to wait in her room unless told otherwise. "You can have one of the other girls bring you something to eat," he said.

Ginny saw her chance to return to her cabin to tend to Scarlet. "Detective Keating, may I return to my cabin for a few moments? I really do need to feed my cat." Would he insist on accompanying her?

He grumbled and waved her on, and Ginny said goodbye to Maureen with a promise to give her more details of the audition soon, and exited.

Ginny noticed Hendrik walking behind her.

"I'll go with you," he insisted.

"I should be fine, Mr. Bergen, but thank you," Ginny said politely.

"I'll just come along. It's a matter of safety."

"Oh, all right," Ginny said.

"That was a very nice thing for you to do for Miss Vix," Hendrik commented. "And good job convincing that Keating fellow not to bring all of us into jail. You're a generous and clever woman. Those are qualities I admire very much."

Ginny felt herself blushing. "Thank you, Mr. Bergen."

6

Scarlet purred behind the cabin door, and Ginny spoke to her through the wood.

"Just another moment, darling."

"Poor thing," Hendrik spoke as he knelt on the floor to comfort the cat through the door. His sympathy for the animal surprised Ginny in a good way.

Ginny opened the door. Scarlet ran to her, and Ginny collected the cat in her arms. Hendrik insisted on checking inside her room before she entered.

"I'm sure I'm not in any danger, really," Ginny said. "Scarlet wouldn't have been so calm if that were the case."

"I'd still like to check just to be sure. With us walking around with the detective before, there's a chance the murderer might have seen you, and who knows what they're thinking. They could imagine you are a witness and saw them."

"You're quite right," Ginny spoke. "I'll wait here." She stroked Scarlet's soft coat. She stood just outside the doorway while Hendrik went inside to look. Scarlet purred at Ginny's touch.

Ginny heard something fall over in her room and clutched Scarlet close to her chest. Had something happened to Hendrik? She wondered whether she should run and get the detective or confront the culprit herself.

Hendrik appeared at the doorway. "All clear. Except I somehow managed to knock over your record player," he said with a grin.

Ginny exhaled in relief. "Thank goodness that's all it was. When I heard the noise, I didn't know what to think."

Hendrik continued to grin. "You were concerned about me?"

"Yes, I quite was, actually," Ginny admitted.

"I'm grateful, Miss Weltermint."

"I wish you would stop with this Miss business, it's ever so formal," Ginny said with a laugh.

"All right, Ginny."

Hendrik sat on the edge of the bed while Ginny shut the door and fed Scarlet and set out fresh water for her. The cat showed her appreciation by nuzzling Ginny's leg and purring. Ginny had put down newspaper for her earlier.

"Do you mind?" Ginny asked Hendrik when she'd finished. "I want to change into fresh clothes."

"Of course." He started to turn around.

"Don't bother," Ginny said, opening the small closet door. "I'll just stand behind this." She grabbed a dress and went behind the door to change.

"Mind if I turn on the record player?" Hendrik asked her.

"Go right ahead," Ginny said.

Scarlet had finished eating and jumped up on the bed but wouldn't sit near Hendrik when he reached out for her. It amused her how the cat seemed to avoid him.

"This is all very exciting, but I never imagined myself being involved in something like this, especially not on my way home," Ginny spoke to Hendrik as she dressed.

"This must be like one of your plots," he said.

"I've always wanted to write a detective picture."

"Set your next one on a train," Hendrik suggested. "It would make a great storyline."

"Say, that isn't a bad idea. I'll have to include a detective character like our friend."

"Keating's straight out of the movies," Hendrik said.

"Or a bad dream," Ginny joked. "He's certainly not my idea of a pulp novel character."

The record player began to play the song that reminded her of Beth, and Ginny asked Hendrik to turn it off.

He did, and she explained to him why.

They were quiet for a few moments until Ginny said, "There, all done," and stepped away from the door and closed it.

"Where to next?" Hendrik said, rising from the bed.

"I have to make a phone call or two," Ginny said. "Remember when I promised Miss Vix I'd speak to my friend out in Hollywood?"

"Shall I come with you?"

"I don't think that's needed, but thank you. I'm sure you have better things to do than follow me around all day."

"I do have some business paperwork I could attend to. But let's meet up later, shall we?"

Ginny nodded. "I'd like that."

Hendrik left the room, and Scarlet sauntered over to the newspaper to do her business while Ginny fixed her hair and makeup. Once she was done, she gestured for Scarlet to go wait on the bed and left her cabin, closing the door.

The train had a public telephone, just off to the side of the aisle near the first-class car, and Ginny went in its direction. When she arrived, she found that many other passengers had had the same idea, and there was a long queue of people waiting for a turn on the telephone. From what Ginny overheard, it seemed many were calling their families or places of work with the news of their delay.

Ginny reasoned Detective Keating couldn't arrange for the passengers to be transferred to another train because the culprit could be among them. She imagined they could be stagnant for at least a few more days until the murder was solved. The detective couldn't keep the passengers on the train for longer than that, as Ginny imagined there were laws against that sort of thing.

Ginny stood in the queue and waited for her turn on the phone. She had two calls to make, so she planned to keep them brief, lest the others waiting think her rude for taking too long. Hendrik really was quite a dreamboat, she thought as she waited. Handsome, attentive, and reliable. She hadn't planned to see him past their trip, but perhaps she could make an exception and spend more time with him in California if he was agreeable.

Ginny didn't know how long she'd been waiting. If she had been wearing her watch, she could have checked. But, as it was, she was without it. When the second-to-last person in front of her ended their phone call to their mother, Ginny believed, she let out a big sigh of relief. One more to go, and she could make her own calls. The man in a hat in front of her made a brief call, then it was her turn. Finally, some good luck had been bestowed on her.

Ginny walked up to the phone booth and spoke to the operator, who connected her to the studio boss Mickey Goldstein out in Hollywood.

Mickey's loud, friendly voice came on the line. "How's my favorite writer? We'll be seeing you in a few days?"

"Mickey," Ginny said. "I have so much to tell you. You see, there's been a murder on the train I'm on, and we've been delayed. Likely, for a few days."

"A murder!" Mickey exclaimed and asked her more about it.

Ginny told him a little more information.

"A murder on a train," Mickey mused out loud. "I like the sound of that. It could be your next picture. What do you say, kid?"

Mickey always called her 'kid' because she was younger than him.

"That's what I was thinking," Ginny said. "I've been trailing the detective on the case. He actually thinks I might be a suspect because I found the body. Isn't that a laugh?"

"You're a suspect? You found the body! This is even better than I thought. So you're right in the middle of the action. That's the inspiration you need."

The woman in the queue behind Ginny cleared her throat as if Ginny was taking too long.

"I'll work up a draft when I get home, Mickey. The real reason I rang you is I want to ask you about this girl I met on the train. She's coming out to Hollywood because she wants to be an actress."

"Is she involved with the murder?"

"I don't think she is. No, she isn't."

"Oh." Mickey sounded disappointed. "You want me to get her an audition?" he asked. He was always one to get straight down to business.

"Yes. She's really quite pretty, and I can just tell she's going to be terrific. She has a certain quality to her that I think you're looking for."

"Sure. She can have an audition. I trust your judgement. What's her name?"

"Maureen Vix."

"I like her name already. You know how important a good name is in show business."

"Yes. Thank you, Mickey. She's going to be great. I just know it. Goodbye now. I have to go." Ginny ended the call before the loquacious Mickey could continue.

Next, Ginny had the operator connect her to her mother's house in the city. The woman behind Ginny seemed exasperated that she hadn't finished yet.

"Mother!" Ginny said when the familiar, warm voice came on the line.

"Ginny," her mother replied. "I didn't expect to hear from you until you arrived in California. Is everything all right?"

"The train had to stop because someone was killed onboard," Ginny explained.

Her mother gasped. "Was it an accident?"

"No, he was murdered, mother."

Ginny could tell the woman waiting for her turn behind her was listening in on her conversation, so she lowered her voice slightly. "I've actually been assisting the detective with the investigation."

"How did that come about?" her mother asked.

"I discovered the body and became involved."

"Oh, my. I do hope it's not dangerous," her mother fretted.

"More dangerous than screenwriting, I suppose." She told her mother a little about Detective Keating. "He's quite an unpleasant man, if you ask me."

"He does sound that way, dear. When do you think the train will be moving again?"

"Once this thing is resolved. At the rate it's going, I don't have much hope that we'll be on our way anytime soon."

"How dreadful for you to have discovered such a horror," her mother said.

"I found it quite exciting, actually."

"Yes, I suppose you would. You are a writer, after all. I do hope you're safe, after discovering the body. You don't know who the killer is, do you?" Her mother spoke as though they were sharing a big secret between them.

"No, I didn't see them, and I don't think they saw me. Besides, I have Hendrik Bergen to thank for my safety."

"Who is he? Another detective?"

"No, he's a man I met aboard. He works for Blue Autos."

"Oh, an executive?"

She imagined her mother thought this meant she was moving on from Paul.

"No, he's an engineer."

"Still, a decent profession."

"Yes, well, he's sort of become my travelling companion. He's been very supportive of me during this ordeal."

"Sounds heroic. Do tell me more about him. Is he handsome?"

"Yes, he's quite good looking."

"Tall?"

"Yes, very."

"Does he seem responsible, or does he have a dash of playboy in him?"

"Mother, let's not get ahead of ourselves here. Hendrik and I aren't even sweet on each other yet – we're just friends."

"Yes, but love can grow out of friendship. Paul has moved on with that girl you knew."

"Beth, her name's Beth."

"Yes, he's moved on with that Beth girl."

"Mother, we already talked about this while I was visiting you. I'm not hung up on Paul any longer."

"I know you'd like to think that, darling, but love is so hard to fall out of."

"I still have feelings for Paul, of course. But I've accepted that he and Beth are a pair, and I wish them the best."

"You're certainly more generous than I would have been in the same situation."

"I don't see the point in hating them. Of course, they'll never be my favorite people."

"Of course not, dear."

"Now, mother, I do have to go. There's a long queue for the phone, and I'm afraid the others will think me terribly rude unless I end our chat very soon."

"All right, dear. Goodbye. Ring me once you reach California. Perhaps I'll read about this train crime in the newspapers."

"If they do write about it, I hope they don't print

my name. After the scandal with Paul, I don't need any more attention put on me, but if they found out about Jake, would it really be the worst thing, mother?"

"I don't like to think it would be, dear. But some are still so old-fashioned these days that the idea of a lady writing cowboys still doesn't sit well with them. You wouldn't want to let your pride, which I admire, jeopardize your career. I'm not sure the day will ever come when we women can be who we desire to be."

Although Ginny knew her mother liked to pride herself as being very modern, like all the women in their family, Ginny felt that her own private take on the matter, one she kept to herself, was still a cut above her mother's. She knew the day would come, and hopefully soon. And that, one day, the public would accept her as Virginia Weltermint, lady writer of Westerns, and not Jake Byrne.

"Yes, mother, you're right, of course," she said to humor her. "I really do have to go, I'm afraid."

"Yes, dear. Goodbye."

"Hi, Ginny," someone said to her right.

She nearly died of fright and turned around to see who had spoken to her.

Hendrik smiled. "I didn't mean to alarm you."

How long had he been standing there, and had he overheard what she'd spoken to her mother about him?

Still, Ginny said, "Hello," with a smile. "Have you finished your paperwork already?" she asked.

"No, but I grew tired of it and decided to go for a walk."

"I'm surprised the detective is letting people move about more," Ginny observed, looking around her. "Although I assumed that would happen eventually. I don't think he can control it. It's much easier to keep people on board than in their places."

"Yes, that's true," Hendrik said.

"My conversation just now," Ginny said. "Did you happen to overhear any of it?"

"No, I just got here."

Ginny couldn't tell whether he was fibbing, but she decided not to press the matter further.

"Would you like to see if we could get a drink in the lounge?" Hendrik asked.

"Have they reopened it?"

"I'm not sure, but we could go see," he suggested.

"I'd love to, in a little while," Ginny said. She needed to speak with Maureen about the audition she'd arranged for her, and there was also something she wanted to talk to the train conductor about.

"Sounds terrific," Hendrik said. "What do you say we meet there in an hour? Perhaps it will be opened by then."

Ginny agreed, and they arranged to meet. She watched him walking away and wondered if her mother could be right about him, but as much as the possibility of romance excited her, she didn't think she could throw herself into anything serious just yet.

7

Ginny went toward the second-class sleeping car in search of Maureen, whom she expected to find in the cabin she shared with the other girls. She felt she'd remembered the girl's room number correctly and knocked on the closed door.

She heard Maureen say, "One moment, please" and the sound of footsteps coming to the door.

"Hi, Maureen," Ginny said as the girl opened the door.

"Ms. Weltermint!" Maureen seemed delighted to see her. "I'm so grateful you're here. I was getting frightened waiting by myself." She motioned for Ginny to enter and closed the door. It seemed the other girls hadn't returned yet.

"Do you know the girls you're rooming with?" Ginny asked Maureen.

Maureen shook her head. "I suspect they put us all together because we're around the same age. I don't know anyone on the train, except for you and Mr. Bergen."

Ginny smiled. "I came because I have some good news to share with you."

Maureen sat on the bed and looked up at her expectantly.

"May I?" Ginny gestured to the bed.

"Yes, please." Maureen patted the area next to her.

Ginny sat down and set her purse in her lap. "I spoke to my friend out in Hollywood; he's a studio boss, and he'd like to have you audition for him."

Maureen leaned forward and embraced her. "Oh, ma'am, I am ever so grateful! Thank you. Thank you. This has to be the nicest thing anyone has ever done for me."

Ginny patted the girl's back. "You're most welcome."

Maureen sat straight. "How can I ever repay you?"

"There's no need to do that," Ginny said. "I'm happy to help." She wrote down the studio's address for the girl. "And remember, once we get to California, if you ever need anything, you know where to find me."

Maureen embraced her again. "Oh, ma'am, I am so grateful."

"Now, remember what I said, enough with this ma'am business. Call me Ginny."

"Ginny," Maureen said with her face turning rose.

"Now, let's talk about that gin. Was it really yours? Do tell."

Maureen looked slightly ashamed and nodded.

"Just when I thought you were an ordinary young girl," Ginny said in jest. "You're really quite exciting."

"My older brother gave it to me as a parting gift," Maureen admitted.

"How swell of him." Ginny smiled. "I think your brother and I would get along."

"Oh, you would. Michael, that's my brother, he's an admirer of the ladies." Maureen blushed.

"Michael and Maureen. I like that. Are you two the only siblings?"

Maureen nodded. "We're very close. My mother and father are immigrants. Strict Catholics, which is why I didn't want my name in the papers."

"My mother's family were Irish immigrants," Ginny said.

The revelation brightened Maureen's eyes. "And you being such a refined, first-class lady."

"Everyone has to start somewhere. That's good advice, so remember that. My mother's family didn't have much money when they came here, but my mother managed to build quite a career for herself as a theatre actress—of course, she had to change her surname—which is where she met my father, an actor himself, and his family owned many theatres, so he did come from some money. But both of them built their careers over time."

"Mr. Bergen mentioned you were related to the Weltermints," Maureen spoke shyly. "But I didn't want to seem impolite by asking you questions about them."

"Oh, Maureen," Ginny said. "That wouldn't have been impolite."

Maureen blushed. "I'll admit I don't know much about acting, although I want to be an actress, but I have heard of your family. Your childhood must have been fantastic. I'm sorry, I don't mean to sound presumptuous. I have no idea what your childhood was like."

"It's all right, Maureen. My childhood was perfectly nice, as I hope yours was as well."

"It was all right, ma'am—I mean, Ginny. Not very exciting, and my parents did have to work a lot. My father is a laborer and my mother works in big houses. My mother saved up enough money for me to take the trip second class, otherwise I'd be in third class. One of the other girls staying with me in here, her beau is one of the crewmen, which is how come she got herself into second class. I worked with my mother at some of the houses before coming on the train, but never saved much money. Despite not having a lot herself, my mother always made sure my brother and I had enough."

Ginny thought of her family's housekeeper, a hardworking woman she was friendly with, and who had a son around Maureen's age.

"She must be proud of you for fulfilling your dreams," Ginny said.

"I believe she is. My father isn't happy about my leaving. He thinks I'll become a fallen woman out in Hollywood."

"Hollywood can be a rough place. I could see why he's concerned. Perhaps ring him or write to him when you get out there and tell him about me, say that you have a friend out there. That might put him more at ease."

"That would please him. You wouldn't mind, ma'am—Ginny?"

"Absolutely not."

After a few moments, Maureen asked, "Are you and Mr. Bergen sweet on each other? Have you known each other long? Oh, to have such a beau. He's such a handsome man, and his accent is lovely." Her face flushed pink.

Ginny smiled at the girl. She didn't want to trouble

her with the story of Paul, so she said, "Hendrik and I are only friends. We just met on the train. I don't know him very well, I'm afraid."

"I believe that could change, if I may say so. As someone who notices these things, it's clear Mr. Bergen has affection toward you. I don't mean to speak out of turn."

"You are a little," Ginny admitted. "But that's okay," she added when she noticed the girl's nervous expression.

"My father says it's something I do," Maureen said quietly. "He also says my mother does it, and that I must have inherited it from her."

"Oh, that doesn't sound like a very nice thing for him to say. I'm sorry to hear that." Ginny pictured the girl's father as a tyrant of sorts.

"That's one of the reasons I wanted to leave home. I would never tell my family that, of course."

Ginny's father, although an altogether decent man, could be critical at times. "My own father was a bit that way," she told the girl.

"Oh, I never would have imagined Mr. Weltermint to be that way. I saw him one time in the theatre, you know, on Broadway, when my mother took my brother and I there for my birthday. Your father, he was marvelous on stage. Imagine having talent like that and being able to not just act but sing and dance as well. I'm sure your mother is just as marvelous as well. I've never seen her, though. Did they ever consider appearing in the talking pictures?"

"That was after their time," Ginny said. "Although I believe they would have if they were born later."

"Did you ever think of becoming an actress?" Maureen asked her thoughtfully.

"No, actually, I didn't. I prefer to be behind the scenes."

"I imagine it's just as exciting," Maureen gushed. "And do you have any siblings, and are they actors or actresses?"

"My brother is studying to be a doctor."

"He must be very smart."

After a moment, Ginny rose with her purse in hand. "I should be going. There's something I have to do. If you're interested, I can sneak you into the first-class lounge if you'd like to meet Hendrik and me there in a little while. I imagine it could reopen soon."

"Would that be all right? I wouldn't want to jeopardize your standing on the train."

"It's no trouble at all. I'm sure they wouldn't even notice."

"Then I might just join you. Thank you for the offer." Maureen smiled warmly.

Ginny said goodbye to the girl and went to see if she could find the conductor. She wanted to find out more about William O'Connor, and he seemed the likely man to ask. She walked through the crowded aisles in search of him. By then, almost everyone seemed to have disobeyed Detective Keating's orders to remain where they were for the time being and had started to move about the train. The policemen were having trouble keeping order. Ginny saw a few passengers attempting to exit the train, but they were stopped by the crewmen. She reckoned she wouldn't find the conductor in his booth since the train was idle, so she kept an eye out for him in the aisles, reasoning he would be helping to maintain order. Earlier, Ginny had heard him reassuring a couple of passengers that they had enough food and beverages to last the delay and then some.

Ginny spotted the tall, burly conductor ahead, conversing with a man in a red necktie. "Conductor!" She grinned and waved. It wouldn't hurt to use a bit of her charm to get what she wanted.

He stopped speaking to the man to return her wave. Ginny paused and waited for her turn to speak with him. She looked out the train window and could see a few policemen gathered around the vicinity of the train, and one of them was speaking with Detective Keating. Just how long did he plan to delay their trip? She imagined that the investigation could take quite some time and that the detective might not finish before they resumed their journey. She wondered whether they'd all be asked to return to the area at some point to resume the investigation or if the detective would collect what he needed from them individually.

After a few moments, the conductor approached her.

"Yes, miss, what can I do for you?" he asked.

"Say, this delay really is dreadful, isn't it?"

"I can assure you that we will have the train moving as soon as the police give us permission to do so."

"Yes, that's what I assumed. But I was wondering if you knew anything more about what's happened – that is, more than the police are telling the passengers."

The conductor looked a bit taken aback. "I'm afraid I can't disclose that, miss."

"Yes, well, I found the body of the man. He was in first class as well."

"Oh, I'm sorry. Did you know him?"

Ginny admitted she didn't. "But I was wondering whether he was with anyone at the time or if he was alone. I just want to make sure there's nothing additional the police should know."

"I've already talked to the police about that," the conductor said. "I've told them what they need to know."

"Well, was he? I promise I won't tell anyone."

The conductor looked at her as though he knew she knew she wasn't supposed to be asking him the question yet was asking it anyway.

"Miss, are you a member of the police?"

Ginny smiled sweetly and shook her head. She batted her eyelashes at the man.

"Then I don't believe I should be sharing such private information with you," he said.

"Oh, it won't hurt anyone to drop a little hint," Ginny said, vexed that her efforts had failed. "Please?"

"Do you promise to leave me in peace if I do?" the conductor asked.

Ginny nodded.

He sighed. "Yes, he was traveling to California alone, miss."

Ginny patted the man's arm. "Thank you."

Detective Keating entered the train and cleared his throat loudly and gestured for all the passengers to pay attention. Everyone stopped and turned to face him and the young policeman at his side.

"We will be reopening the lounge in order to maintain civility among you," he announced.

"When can we step off this train?" a man shouted from the back of the car.

"As soon as we have solved the murder," Keating replied.

"How long is that going to take?" a woman with an irritated expression asked from her seat. "I have someplace I need to be."

"Yes, everyone has somewhere they need to be," Detective Keating said. "I would hope that doing your public duty to assist the police takes precedence over those other matters."

"I have business I need to attend to," a heavyset man countered near the detective. "If this delay will cut into my income, then I don't care about any duty I might have." He rose from his seat.

"Sir, I ask you to please remain calm," the detective said.

Other passengers started to grumble, and Ginny debated whether to intervene on the detective's behalf. It wouldn't hurt to get on the detective's good side if she wanted to remain a part of the investigation for research into her new picture. After all, once Ginny became focused on something, she never gave up.

She strode up to the detective, and he gave her a perplexed look. She gestured to him that it was all right. Ginny faced her fellow passengers and motioned for them to be quiet.

"Now, I know each and every one of you is exhausted and wants us to be on our way. I understand entirely because I feel the same way. But Detective Keating really is doing all he can to hurry this along, and we all need to be patient for just a bit longer. The job of the police truly is a complex one, and we need to offer them our support in this instance."

A few of the passengers clapped, and someone whistled. Ginny saw Hendrik grinning at her from the back. She turned to her left and was surprised that Detective Keating appeared to be blushing with appreciation. He gave her a swift nod, and Ginny thought that would have to do for now.

A porter opened the door to the lounge, and many passengers rushed to enter to gather and relax. Hendrik went over to her.

"That was a fabulous speech you gave," he said with a grin.

Ginny thanked him.

"I gather our Detective Keating was grateful?" Hendrik said in a jokey way.

"As much as a man like him could be."

"Shall we go get a drink before they run out? I do wish Prohibition wasn't still in effect. I could really use something strong. Do you think Keating's got rid of Maureen's bathtub gin?" he asked with a big smile.

"Normally, I would say that perhaps he's helped himself to it, but he doesn't seem more relaxed," she told Hendrik. "People who would know have told me that Prohibition might end soon."

"I hope they're correct. I've actually considered returning to Europe, I'm so tired of this country being dry."

"We shall have to write to the President and tell him," Ginny said with humor. "We wouldn't want to lose a good man like yourself."

They had to wait in the queue to enter the lounge, and by the time they got inside, there was only one table vacant. Ginny and Hendrik made a dash to claim it before anyone else could.

"Phew." Ginny sat down and exhaled.

Hendrik sat across from her. "I'm glad we can

spend some time together without the company of the detective."

"I'll say…"

Ginny spotted Detective Keating wandering about the lounge. He seemed to be looking for a place to sit and perhaps have a drink, but there were none available, and he cast a glance in the direction of Hendrik and Ginny every so often.

"Should we ask him if he'd like to join us?" Ginny asked Hendrik.

"I'm not sure," he mused. "Are we really in the mood for his kind of company? I don't think he'd make very good company if we want to relax."

"Wouldn't it be rude not to? I believe he's noticed us sitting here. We do have three chairs, and it seems a shame not to share."

Hendrik reluctantly agreed, and Ginny waved to the detective. He approached their table. With his compact stature and thick grey mustache, he did look a bit like a little dog, Ginny thought with a smile. Of course, she would never tell him that.

8

"Is there something I can do for you, miss?" the detective asked Ginny. "You haven't called me over here to inform me that you have solved the death on your own, have you?"

Had he just made a joke? Ginny believed so. In his own way.

"No, detective," she said with a smile. "Would you like to join us?"

He looked from her to Hendrik, who smiled politely, and seemed to be deciding whether he'd like to have them as company.

When he didn't form an answer, Ginny said, "I take it you're searching for a place to sit and relax for a bit, perhaps have a drink? Please, join us. You're very welcome to."

Detective Keating appeared confused that they'd offered him a seat, and Ginny imagined that, given the man's attitude, kindness didn't come often to him.

Hendrik gestured for him to have a seat.

"There is work to be done, and I don't have the time to spare," Detective Keating grumbled.

"You ought to relax for a while, why, with all the hard work you're doing," Ginny said.

He gave her a look as though he couldn't tell if she was being sarcastic.

"All Ginny meant was, why not join us for a few moments?" Hendrik said. "It couldn't hurt to get to know one another better."

Keating put his fingers to his lips, as though thinking, and gave them a short nod. "Yes, well, at the very least, it will be good to make sure the train is not serving alcohol on the sly," he said as he sat down. "I've heard many stories of that happening on board these trains." He didn't seem capable of admitting that he might enjoy their company.

"I can assure you that, unfortunately, they do not serve such drinks on this train," Ginny said with cheek.

Hendrik chuckled.

Keating gave her an open-mouth stare and frowned. "I do not find that very funny, miss, when both of you know very well about Miss Vix's...indiscretion."

"What did you do with it, anyway?" Hendrik asked him with a tinge of humor in his voice. "You had said you would dispose of it."

The detective seemed shocked at the implication that he would do anything with it except that.

"And that is exactly what I did with it, Mr. Bergen," he said.

"That's too bad," Hendrik said with a wink.

"It is every day that I am thankful for Prohibition," Keating remarked.

Hendrik looked across at Ginny, and they smiled secretly at each other.

"And every day I hope it will end," Hendrik replied.

"As an officer of the law, I do not appreciate your tone, sir," the detective said with a frown.

If Ginny had thought that the point of them having a drink with the detective was to get to know him better in a social way, it didn't appear to be heading in that direction. Seeing this, Ginny quickly changed the subject.

"Have you lived in the village for a long time, detective?" she asked. "I know you mentioned your family was from Pennsylvania. The village seems like a very pleasant place, from what I've seen through the windows."

Detective Keating actually smiled at her compliment. "Yes, I've lived here for quite some time. My wife's family is from the village, which is why we settled here. It is a pleasant place."

"How long have you been married?" Hendrik asked, seeming to comprehend Ginny's move.

Keating squinted at him, and Ginny wondered if he ever smiled on a regular basis. "I've been married for nearly forty years. That's not something you young people of your generation can comprehend," he scolded.

"Do you have any children?" she asked him to perhaps lighten the mood.

"Yes, three daughters, all grown," the detective said after a pause.

"They must be lovely," Ginny said. "Are they married or in school?"

"They all work, and one is engaged to be married in the autumn. Advanced schooling is something none of them had interest in, and regardless, it wasn't an expense I could consider on a policeman's pay."

Ginny understood that his words held an underlying criticism of her social class.

"My family did not come from money, and yet I managed to study engineering," Hendrik spoke up, almost in her defense.

"That's something to be congratulated about," the detective said cordially to Ginny's surprise.

"Your daughters must be fascinated by your work," Ginny told Keating.

"No, it doesn't interest them, or my wife," he replied.

"Is that so?" Ginny said.

The few waiters were circling about the car, which sparkled with crystal glasses, fulfilling the wishes of the many passengers, and Hendrik finally got the attention of one of them. He went over to their table, and all three ordered glasses of tonic water.

"A good choice," Ginny said with a smile at Detective Keating, who gave her a civil nod.

The waiter returned with their tonic waters, with a wedge of bright lemon on the edge of each glass. Ginny inquired about snacks.

"I'm afraid the cook is resting at the moment, but we do have some light refreshments to offer," the waiter replied.

All three took him up on his offer. As the waiter strode away, Detective Keating said, "I really ought to finish my drink and return to my duties." His stomach rumbled.

"You ought to have something to eat first," Hendrik said.

"I guess I could spare a few more moments."

"Absolutely," Hendrik said. "Nobody's going to notice if we're stuck for a couple of extra minutes."

"What is your first name, detective, if I may ask?" Ginny asked Keating.

"I'm not certain we're on a first-name basis, given that I haven't officially cleared you of suspicion..."

"You're still going on about that?" Hendrik came to Ginny's defense.

"I can assure you and Miss Weltermint that it is nothing personal," Keating said. "It is merely how I carry out an investigation, by process of elimination, and I have not eliminated her yet or Miss Vix for that matter."

"I don't know about Miss Vix—she seems like a nice girl—but Ginny's clearly done nothing wrong," Hendrik said.

"Yes, we've gone over all this before," the detective replied.

Ginny reached across the table and touched Hendrik's warm hand. "It's all right," she told him.

Detective Keating raised an eyebrow as though he was uncertain about how Hendrik would reply.

"You're right, of course," Hendrik said with a smile at Ginny.

"And my first name is Bartholomew, miss," the detective told Ginny.

"Bartholomew?" Ginny marveled. "How wonderful."

Keating cleared his throat. "Yes, well, my wife has always said it is a very noble name."

"Indeed," Hendrik said.

The waiter returned to their table with a tray of assorted nuts and crackers and cheese. Both Hendrik and Ginny had missed out on the sandwiches offered earlier, as had Detective Keating, Ginny assumed.

To Ginny's surprise, the detective swallowed the last of his drink and rose. "I should be going. There is a murder to be solved."

"You aren't staying to eat?" Ginny said.

"I'm afraid not, miss. I am pressed for time, and I really shouldn't be seen socializing with someone who is still under suspicion."

Ginny knew he meant her.

"I am sorry, miss," he offered.

She and Hendrik stood up and saw him off.

"Well, there's more for us to eat, then," Hendrik said as the detective walked away and they sat down again. "He really is getting a bit carried away with this suspicion business."

Ginny waved off Hendrik's concern. "It will be cleared up in no time. I don't really think he's serious, actually."

Hendrik lit a cigarette. "He might not have much to go on besides you and Miss Vix."

Ginny took out a cigarette also, and Hendrik lit it for her. "Say, do you think the detective smokes?" she bantered, wanting to change the subject because it made her nervous.

"Maybe a pipe on occasion. I doubt he engages in an everyday vice like cigarettes," Hendrik said with a grin.

Ginny had kept a lookout for Maureen, but as far as she knew, the girl never appeared. She'd been looking for her expectant face in the doorway.

"I offered for Maureen to join us," Ginny said. "Only I haven't seen her."

"That was nice of you to do, but I doubt they

would have let her inside, given that the lounge is only for first-class passengers."

"I told her we'd figure out a way to sneak her in," Ginny told him.

"I like that we're conspiring together now," Hendrik said with a grin.

"It's nice," Ginny admitted. "I don't think she's going to show," she said after a moment. "Oh, well, it would have been fun trying."

They ate their snacks with relish and ordered a second round of tonic drinks.

"I'm sure you already know all there is to know about my family from the newspapers," Ginny told him. "How about your family?"

"I'm not married, if that's what you're asking," Hendrik said with a sparkle in his eye.

Ginny had assumed so, but she had never looked for a ring and was relieved to hear his confirmation.

"Divorced? Children?" she asked, but would it matter if he answered yes?

"No children, and not divorced. And I'm assuming you aren't either?"

Ginny nodded. "Paul, my former fiancé—I just realized I've never asked you if you've heard of him."

"I don't believe so," Hendrik said.

"His name is big in dance out in Hollywood. Anyway, he would have been my first marriage. He didn't want children, although according to what I read in the papers, he and his fiancée, my former friend, plan to start a family."

Hendrik shook his head and offered her a sympathetic pat on the hand. "I'm sorry, Ginny."

Ginny shrugged. "I thought I knew him well. Obviously, he wasn't who I thought he was."

"It's such a shame when that happens," Hendrik said, and Ginny detected a tinge of sadness in his voice.

"You sound like you know from experience," she said.

"Not really," Hendrik said quickly. "But I've seen similar things happen to others."

Ginny nodded in understanding. "What about your family?" she asked after a moment. "Any siblings?"

He told her about his Dutch childhood and how his parents were deceased and he had no siblings. She was saddened to hear he was an orphan.

"I'm sorry to hear that, Hendrik," she said.

"It was many years ago, feels like a lifetime ago." After a pause, he said, "I was engaged once, too, years ago."

Ginny wanted to ask what had transpired to end it but didn't want to come across as too forward. She waited for him to disclose it instead, and if he didn't, well, then she would just drop the subject.

"I thought we were in love, but it fell apart in the end," he said after a while. "She wasn't who I thought she was."

"That sounds like what happened with Paul and me," Ginny offered.

"We have something in common. I really do enjoy spending time with you, Ginny."

He held her gaze for so long that Ginny felt a flutter in her stomach.

"And I like spending time with you," she said softly. Perhaps her mother had been right after all, and she and Hendrik might have a future beyond her idea of them spending time in California during his stay there. But after what happened with Paul, she didn't want to rush into things.

"We should arrange to meet up when you're in California," she suggested.

"I'd like that. I might not have too much time to spare, but I can spare some," he said, and she was a bit disappointed.

"Well, if you have time," she said, not wanting to sound desperately eager.

"Sure, I will," he said. "I'm staying just outside of Hollywood."

She gave him her address, and he wrote it down, which made their plans seem more definite. "I can show you around the area," she said. "Assuming this train ever continues to move. I should have some time available over the following days after our arrival."

"Terrific. I'll look forward to it."

Yet, there was a certain tone in his voice that made her question whether it would actually occur. What was going on, exactly?

"Is everything all right?" she asked.

"Yes, yes. I just remembered I have more to do once we arrive than I thought." He sighed.

"Oh?" she said. "That's too bad."

"Of course we can spend some time together," he asserted. "And you should also come visit me in New York some time."

There it was again, the tone in his voice. Why was she doubting him? Perhaps she was being overly sensitive after Paul's broken promises.

She tried to sound enthusiastic. "I'd like that."

Hendrik looked at his watch. "Say, it's later than I thought. I best be going. I need to finish up some business. I very much enjoyed our drink."

Why did she think he sounded eager to leave? What was going on? Then again, maybe she was being too touchy given the situation with Paul.

"I did as well," she said. "I am tired. I think I'll return to my cabin to rest for a while. I haven't slept a wink."

"I'm surprised you're still standing," Hendrik said with a smile.

He signaled for the check, and the waiter came to the table with it.

"Shall I walk with you to your cabin?" he asked Ginny.

"Thank you, but that's quite all right." She didn't want to be tempted to ask him to stay.

Hendrik paid the bill, and Ginny thanked him. They rose and parted ways at the doorway. Scarlet would be eagerly awaiting her return.

Ginny walked through the various cars and heard Detective Keating's loud voice somewhere in the nearby vicinity. She truly hoped that he would clear up this being suspicious of her business soon. It was getting tiresome, and it also unsettled her.

Ginny reached her cabin and found the door ajar. She realized she hadn't locked it. But how had it gotten open? And the sound of music, her music, drifted out of the room. She trusted Scarlet enough not to venture out of the room, but it still concerned her because it wasn't as she remembered leaving it. She certainly hadn't left her record player on.

She noticed a short-statured porter cleaning the windows in the area outside her room.

Ginny went up to the pale man. "Did you notice someone entering my room?" She indicated which cabin was hers.

Scripted Murder

He didn't look at her but briefly looked in the direction of her room and shook his head. Then he returned to his work.

Ginny thought about whether to press the matter further with him, but he seemed determined to ignore her. Perhaps he was just very devoted to the task at hand, which she found strange given the fact that they weren't even moving yet, or he was hiding something. Ginny suspected the latter. But what might it be?

9

Ginny returned to her cabin and slowly pushed the door open all the way. Scarlet purred at her from the bed, and she breathed out in relief. She could hear the music clearly once inside the room, and the song playing was the one that reminded her of Beth. Ginny shivered as she quickly turned off the record. She gingerly looked around the room to see if anything was out of place and noticed little was changed except for what looked like a slip of paper had been left on the little table behind her.

She went over and picked up the note and read it closely.

It's best to mind your own business.

The message sounded threatening. The handwriting was carefully formed, and she didn't recognize it. Ginny gasped and dropped the note to the floor. Someone wanted to frighten her. But who? The murderer. Somehow, they knew who she was. They might have been in the vicinity when she discovered the body. Maureen. Could it have been her? Or could it have been the Warwicks? She didn't know either particularly well but didn't like to think them capable of murder. But perhaps one of them was. She hadn't seen any of them at the lounge earlier, so who knew what they were doing during that time.

That porter might have seen someone enter her cabin. Ginny picked up the note and walked swiftly out of her room and shut the door to keep Scarlet inside. She marched over to where the man was still cleaning the windows and held the note out to him.

"Pardon me, do you know who left this in my cabin?" she asked politely.

He kept shaking his head. "No, miss. I'm sorry, I know nothing of the sort."

Ginny glanced at his nametag and saw the name "Smith."

"Are you sure, Mr. Smith? Because it would really be a help to me if you remembered anything. Even the slightest thing could be of assistance." She gave him her best smile.

He wouldn't meet her gaze and just shook his head. "No, miss. I'm sorry, I didn't see anything."

"You didn't see anything, anything at all? Are you sure? Did you notice if someone went into my room, someone who wasn't me?" She tried to encourage him to answer her.

This time, his tone was a bit sharper. "No, miss. As I said before, I noticed nothing of the sort."

Oh, well. If only Scarlet could talk!

Something occurred to Ginny. What if the porter himself had something to do with the note being left there? To confront the man directly would seem boorish, so she would have to find Detective Keating to do it for her.

"Very well," she said to the man in a sharper tone herself.

Ginny locked her door and took off with the note in her hand in search of Detective Keating. She wouldn't allow anyone to frighten her into not pursuing her curiosity about who killed Mr. O'Connor. If whoever had put the note there had thought they could scare her, they were absolutely incorrect.

Ginny walked swiftly along the corridor and into the sitting area and down the aisle. She saw Detective Keating speaking with Hendrik in the area of the smoking car.

She stopped walking and overheard Hendrik ask Keating, "Say, just how serious are you about Ginny Weltermint being a suspect in this mess?"

"Since Miss Weltermint and Miss Vix both discovered the body, they are still both suspects for the time being. I promise you that you'll be the first to know as soon as that changes."

Ginny appreciated that Hendrik was looking out for her, but part of her felt that he was becoming a bit too involved since they didn't know each other all that well.

Hendrik noticed her and waved her over.

"Ginny, we were just talking about you," he said.

"Really? How interesting. I do hope it was a good conversation."

"Indeed, it was very enlightening," Hendrik replied.

Detective Keating murmured, "Yes, certainly."

"I thought you had work to do," Ginny said to Hendrik.

"I decided it could wait a little while," he said.

Ginny reasoned that he had sought out the detective to ask him about her.

"Detective," Ginny said, holding the note out to

him. "Something strange has happened to me, and I thought I ought to tell you about it."

Keating looked down at the note she held and seemed disinterested.

"This was left in my cabin. The door wasn't locked, and they must have put it there while I was with Hendrik in the lounge. It's actually quite threatening, as you can see." She moved the note closer to within his eyesight.

"Oh, did they?" Detective Keating said in amusement. "Perhaps your cat can be a witness."

He sounded as though he thought she had fabricated the scenario and written the note herself!

"I can assure you that I am not making this up." Ginny reached into her purse and produced a *To Do* list she had written for herself in New York. She showed both notes to the detective. "As you can see, the handwriting is clearly different from mine."

"Surely, she is correct," Hendrik chimed in.

"Hmm," the detective said. "May I?" He reached for both notes.

She nodded, and he took them from her and studied them carefully. After a few moments, he handed Ginny's list back to her but kept the note for himself.

"It would seem you are correct," Detective Keating admitted to Ginny. "It could have been left by the killer. Did you see anyone in the vicinity of your cabin?"

"Only a porter," Ginny said. "Named Smith. And he acted quite cagey when I asked him about it."

"I shall like to speak with him," Keating said and headed off to the sleeping car.

Ginny followed with Hendrik by her side.

"Are you all right?" he asked her thoughtfully as they walked.

"I'm a bit alarmed," Ginny said. "The murderer must know who I am, and they don't seem to like what they feel is my digging around for the truth."

"It could be someone you know, or someone who's seen you with the detective."

"Someone such as Maureen or the Warwicks, although I don't like to think them capable of such a thing."

"Very true," Hendrik said. "And I don't believe I saw them in the lounge."

"We know Mr. O'Connor had arranged to meet Maureen, but how could the Warwicks be connected to him?"

"I'm not sure," Hendrik said. "We'll have to find out."

They reached the sleeping car and her cabin door. The porter's cleaning supplies were there, but he was nowhere to be seen.

"I'll check down there for him," Hendrik said, approaching the other end of the corridor.

Keating nodded and went the other way.

Ginny remained by her door in case the porter appeared.

After a few minutes, both men returned, unsuccessful.

"I would like to have a look in your room," Detective Keating told Ginny. "In case they left a clue."

Ginny nodded and unlocked her door for him.

"After you," she said, gesturing for him to enter, followed by her and Hendrik.

Scarlet meowed at the detective from the bed, and

to Ginny's surprise, he went over and she allowed him to stroke her without protest.

"I've always liked cats," Keating remarked.

She and Hendrik looked at each other, as though both were surprised by his kindness.

"It's good to meet a fellow cat lover," Ginny said.

"She won't let me pet her for some reason," Hendrik said.

Detective Keating eyed Ginny and said, "I have no idea why that would be," and Ginny saw a hint of a smile forming on his lips, as though he had attempted to crack a joke between them. Hendrik hadn't seemed to notice.

Ginny smiled to herself at the secret exchange between herself and the detective.

"Nothing seems to be out of place," she told him after a moment.

"Yes, well, I shall look regardless," Keating said as he knelt and checked under the bed on his hands and knees.

"I don't think he's hiding under there," Hendrik said, and Ginny suppressed a giggle.

Detective Keating rose to his feet and frowned at him. He dusted off his hands on his trousers and strode about her rather small room, as though determined to prove them wrong. Ginny and Hendrik waited quietly for him. He opened the curtain and looked out the window at his policemen watching the exits below, as though checking to see if it was possible for them to have noticed something amiss from outside. He shook his head, and after a few moments, faced them.

"It appears you are right, Miss Weltermint," he said to her. "Now, the question is, where do we find the porter you claim to have seen, and once, and if, we are able to locate him, does he indeed know anything as you suspect?"

From his words, it appeared he was questioning whether she had actually seen the man like she had claimed. Ginny reasoned she should be grateful he even believed her about the note.

"I can assure you I haven't invented this porter," she told the detective. "He was here, cleaning the windows outside my cabin—his supplies are still there." She indicated to the corridor outside. "And he acted quite strange when I attempted to speak with him. He would not look me in the eye and kept polishing the windows."

"Yes, it does sound quite strange," Keating said. "But perhaps he was just trying to work and you were interfering with his work. What if he isn't our culprit, then who else could it be?"

Ginny told Detective Keating her theory about Maureen Vix and the Warwicks. "I don't like to suspect any of them, of course, but they weren't in the lounge during that time and could have easily gone into my room."

"Very well," Keating replied. "Let's go find them, shall we?"

He marched out of her room, and Ginny shut and locked the door. Once again, they followed the detective down the corridor, this time to the Warwicks' cabin. Ginny didn't know whether to expect to find them there or if they had gone out, but she recalled that Mrs. Warwick had been ill.

Detective Keating knocked on their door, and when Mr. Warwick inquired who it was, the detective announced himself.

Mr. Warwick opened the door wearing his eyeglasses.

"Good day, sir, I'm afraid it's me again." The detective attempted a meager smile.

"Yes, I can see that," Mr. Warwick said. He gestured to Ginny and Hendrik. "What's this all about?"

"Miss Weltermint has found a rather sinister note left for her in her cabin."

"Yes, well, how terrible, but I don't see why that has anything to do with us," Mr. Warwick replied with a sympathetic nod at Ginny.

"I'd like to see a sample of you and your wife's handwriting."

Mr. Warwick's jaw dropped and he clutched his chest. "Are you implying that one of us might have left it?"

"Not at all, sir, but I need to check just in case. The truth of the matter is that you were in the vicinity of where the body was found, you know that it was Miss Weltermint who discovered it, and you were not in the lounge at the time the note was found."

"How do you know we weren't there?" Mr. Warwick asked the detective.

"I was there, sir."

"Yes, he was having a drink with us," Hendrik said.

"So, that's how it is. You three are all friendly now? I don't like the implication one bit, you ganging up on us. My wife and I have done nothing of the sort."

"I beg your pardon, sir, but if you have nothing to hide, then why not allow us to enter and produce a writing sample for you and your wife?" Detective Keating asked.

Mr. Warwick grumbled in exasperation and held

open the door for them. "Do you mind? My wife is resting. I really don't appreciate her being disturbed."

"I remember she's been ill," Ginny said sympathetically as they entered. "I'm sorry to hear she still isn't feeling well."

Mr. Warwick closed the door. "Which is why this makes your timing all the worse."

"We do apologize for the inconvenience," Hendrik said.

"I do hope this was all his idea and not yours," Mr. Warwick said, gesturing to the detective.

Ginny smiled sheepishly at the man, who frowned at her reaction.

Mrs. Warwick sat up in bed and groggily inquired to her husband what was happening. "What are all these people doing in our room, dear?"

"It's all right, dear," her husband told her. He glanced at Ginny and Hendrik. "I don't see why all of you have to be here."

"Yes, well, the note was left for Miss Weltermint," the detective replied.

"And what about him?" Mr. Warwick looked at Hendrik.

"He's here for support," Ginny answered fast.

"Support? Two civilians following a detective? I've never heard of such a thing," Mr. Warwick grumbled.

Ginny began to think her idea hadn't been a good one. But soon Mr. Warwick settled, and the detective explained to him and his wife what he needed from them.

"I'm afraid we don't have any paper to write on," Mrs. Warwick said. "We do have a pencil somewhere in my luggage." She started to get out of bed, but her husband stopped her.

"Don't stress yourself, dear. I'll look for it."

Mr. Warwick found the pencil, and Detective Keating took out his notepad and tore off two sheets of paper. He asked the Warwicks to print their names on the paper, which Mrs. Warwick did from the bed while leaning the paper against a book.

Mr. Warwick leaned against the small table near the door and finished first and handed the paper to the detective.

"Now you can see for yourself that it doesn't look familiar," he spoke with slight annoyance.

Detective Keating murmured, "We shall see," and grasped the slip of paper. He held both up to the light, comparing the two. "It would seem you are correct."

Mrs. Warwick finished writing her name, and her husband fetched it from her in the bed and gave it to the detective.

"You will see that my wife is innocent also. How could she have left the note if she's been in bed this whole time?" Mr. Warwick spoke with indignation.

Detective Keating took the paper. Again, he held both up to the light. He took more time with Mrs. Warwick's sample, and after a moment, he seemed satisfied and declared, "It seems this sample doesn't match the note either."

"As I said," Mr. Warwick replied, gloating in the fact that he'd been correct. "Now, if you'll excuse us, my wife needs to return to her rest."

Ginny apologized as they left the room, but Mr. Warwick didn't seem to hear.

"Where to next?" Hendrik said in the corridor.

"I suppose we should find Maureen," Ginny said.

"Yes, well, I only need to find her. You really don't

need to trail me around like this," Detective Keating spoke, seeming to recall Mr. Warwick's remark.

Wanting to continue to be part of the investigation, Ginny ignored his comment in the hope that he would overlook his own words and was pleased to see Hendrik doing the same. The detective trudged down the corridor toward second class, and Ginny and Hendrik had to walk fast to match his pace.

10

They stood behind Detective Keating as he knocked on Maureen's door. Another girl, Ginny recognized as one she'd seen playing cards, answered, keeping the door partly closed.

"I am here to see Maureen Vix," Detective Keating said with a clearing of his throat.

"Maureen, you have some visitors. I think one of them is a policeman," the girl spoke to Maureen inside.

Ginny heard Maureen yawning. "You can let them in, Cecilia."

Cecilia, a plump, black-haired girl, opened the door all the way. Ginny entered with Detective Keating and Hendrik. Maureen rose from the bed where she'd been resting in her day clothes.

"It looks like we disturbed your nap," Ginny said with a smile. Evening was approaching, and Ginny could see the sun setting through the window in the girls' cabin.

"What's going on?" Maureen asked.

"The detective has something he'd like to talk with you about," Hendrik said.

"I can speak for myself, thank you," Keating told him.

"I'm sorry I didn't join you and Mr. Bergen at the lounge earlier," Maureen said to Ginny with a shy smile. "I fell asleep, and Cecilia forgot to wake me up."

"She sleeps like a log," Cecilia said.

"That's quite all right, Maureen," Ginny replied.

"We missed your company," Hendrik added.

"What's this, I hear? You were planning to go to the first-class lounge, when you aren't in first class?" Detective Keating questioned the girl. "The lot of you should know that's against the rules," he said, looking at all three of them.

"With all due respect, sir, you went into the lounge with us, and you aren't even a passenger," Hendrik said.

"That's different, I am a police officer," Keating said.

"Pardon me, but I don't see how it's really all that different," Hendrik replied.

"Neither do I, I'm afraid," Ginny said.

"I can assure you it is different," the detective replied with an air of superiority. "Now, where were we? Miss Vix," he said, turning to her. "You are going to need to produce a sample of your handwriting so that I can compare it. Miss Weltermint received a rather peculiar note and, as a formality, I've been asking some of the passengers to write their names for me to assess."

"Oh, no!" Maureen said, looking at Ginny with her mouth open. "That sounds awful for you, ma'am—I mean, Ginny."

"Yes, it was rather alarming," Ginny replied. "I'm sorry that you have to be troubled with this, Maureen, and I don't want you to feel put in a difficult place."

"That's all right, miss. After everything you've done for me, I'm happy to do whatever I can to help."

She really was being a good sport about it, considering, compared with Mr. Warwick.

"Yes, certainly after the discovery of that prohibited drink, you can see why I came to you," Detective Keating said, and Ginny felt he risked ruining the girl's comfort with the situation.

Maureen looked at her feet. "I am sorry about that, sir."

"Good, good," Detective Keating said. "Do you have paper to write on, or do I have to waste another piece of mine?"

"I have a blank journal my mother gave me for the trip," Maureen said, walking to a suitcase and opening it on the floor. She took out a leather-bound journal and pencil and brought them over with her.

"What do you need me to write, sir?" she asked the detective. She dropped the pencil on the floor and picked it up. Ginny thought she seemed nervous now.

"I need you to write your name, miss," Keating said to Maureen.

"Every actress needs to practice their autograph signature," Ginny said to ease Maureen.

"Oh, yes, that's right." Maureen balanced the journal against her knee and scribbled her name down quickly. She showed the results to Detective Keating.

It seemed to Ginny that he took much time assessing it alongside the note Ginny had received. Maureen peeked over his shoulder, trying to read the note Ginny received.

Detective Keating finished his evaluation. "I'm afraid your handwriting is quite similar to the handwriting on the note," he told Maureen.

"Oh, it can't be!" she said in horror.

"She wrote her name very fast," Ginny countered in defense of Maureen. "Are you very sure it's similar?"

"It is quite." He showed both to her.

There was a similarity, although Ginny didn't think it as strong as the detective had suggested. Hendrik took a look also and murmured, "Interesting." Then he said, "But I have to agree with Ginny that Maureen wrote her name quite quickly. Couldn't that have skewed the results?"

"It's possible," Detective Keating agreed. "But in my experience, it is unlikely."

Maureen gasped, and when she looked at Ginny, her eyes were lined with red and shining with tears. "I didn't leave the note in your room, miss. I swear I didn't."

"No one mentioned it was left inside her room," Keating remarked.

"It was an easy enough assumption for her to make," Ginny said.

"I agree. I would have made it myself," Hendrik said.

"Enough," Detective Keating said. "Allow me to think." He put his finger to his lips and stayed quiet. After a moment, he said, "The handwriting is quite similar. What do you have to say for yourself, Miss Vix?" He eyed her.

"I didn't do anything," she said, with tears still creating a sheen in her eyes.

Suddenly, Cecilia, who had been silently watching

the exchange occur, interjected. "She couldn't have done it," she told the detective.

Keating faced her. "And why is that, miss?" He seemed flustered by the interruption.

"Because she hasn't left the room for hours. We've been in here together the whole time, sir, while the other girls have gone out. Maureen's been sleeping. I've been reading." She pointed to a book on one of the bunk beds.

"You're providing an alibi for Miss Vix?" he asked. "Why didn't you speak moments ago? You do know it is a very serious offense to lie to the police, young lady."

"Yes, sir, I am aware of that. I'm not lying," Cecilia said. "I only spoke up just now because I didn't want to interrupt you. Pardon my delay."

Ginny thought the girl seemed quite intelligent.

Detective Keating seemed to be searching over the girl's face to gauge her credibility. "Where are you from, miss?" he asked. "Why are you traveling to California?"

"I'm meeting my brother out there," Cecilia answered. "He's older, and he's been working out there for a few years now on a farm, and he's found me a job. I'm from Long Island, and my family are potato farmers."

"Why are you traveling to California to work on a farm if your family already does so right here in New York?"

"It'd be a better position for me. I'd be working as a supervisor instead of on the farm itself."

"And how is it that you ended up in second class?" Detective Keating asked.

"My brother sent me the money, sir. He's a manager on a big farm," Cecelia told him. "One of the girls staying here is traveling to be a secretary in California. I don't know why the other girl is traveling. Her beau is one of the crewmen."

"All four of you young ladies are traveling without escorts?" he asked, as though it were improper.

Ginny came to the girl's defense, "They are young ladies, not children."

"Yes, well, such a thing would have never occurred in my day. It would have been considered indecent."

"It's a good thing we aren't in your day any longer, detective," Ginny remarked, and Hendrik chuckled.

Detective Keating frowned at her. "Just why exactly have you and Mr. Bergen been following me around? There really is no need for your presence any longer."

"I found the note, and I'd like to help find out who left it there for me," Ginny said. "Hendrik's here for support."

"Support?"

"Yes, that's right," Hendrik said.

Keating grumbled and returned his attention to the two girls. "I have no way to confirm whether either of you is lying, so I will have to just take your word for it. Do you both promise me you are being truthful? As I've said, lying to the police is a very serious matter," he told them.

"I am. And Cecelia's also telling you the truth, sir," Maureen replied.

"I am, sir. Maureen's been here with me," Cecelia said.

"It would seem that the handwriting is merely similar," Detective Keating declared. "Now, unless there's anything else you would like to share with me, I shall be on my way."

Both girls shook their heads. "No, sir," they both said.

"Thank you for your time, ladies," he said to them and proceeded to leave. Then he stopped and turned around. He looked at both Maureen and Ginny.

"You are still under suspicion," he stated.

Hendrik shook his head in frustration, and Ginny asked the detective, "What about the Warwicks?"

"I've concluded it's unlikely," he replied.

Ginny and Hendrik followed him outside. She apologized to Maureen for the inconvenience on her way out.

"I'm not angry, ma'am—Ginny."

"I'm glad to hear it," Ginny said with a smile.

"Where to next?" Hendrik spoke over Keating's shoulder. He seemed just as eager as she was to clear her name once and for all.

"I don't know about you, but I am going to see if I can find that porter Smith Miss Weltermint claims to have seen."

"I did see him," Ginny said. "He was working right outside my room. You saw his supplies yourself."

"I saw someone's supplies; I did not see a man. I have no idea who they belonged to," the detective said.

"Of course they belonged to a workman aboard the train," Hendrik said.

"Yes, some workman, I'm not sure if he was a porter."

"He most certainly was," Ginny said, sighing at his logic.

The detective shook his head in frustration at her

but dropped the matter. "Regardless, I shall see if I can find this man you claim to have seen."

The walk through the corridors and aisles of the immobile train seemed to Ginny to take a long time. A few passengers stopped Detective Keating to inquire when they would be moving again, and, with a sheen of perspiration on his brow, he brushed them off. Ginny saw the conductor, who was barely maintaining order in the place, in one of the aisles. It seemed many people had reached their breaking point and wanted to leave—now, and Ginny sensed that the detective felt pressure to solve the murder as soon as possible. She hoped such urgency wouldn't cause him to make a rash maneuver and blame someone just for the sake of solving it. But she also felt that the detective, although his suspicion of her was unfounded, was an upright man who would avoid such an outcome.

Ginny caught sight of a man hiding behind the doorway of the still-closed dining car and pointed him out to the detective.

"Look at that man."

"Yes, what about him? Do you recognize him? Is he the man you saw?"

"I'm not sure. I'll need to have a closer look."

"Very well," Detective Keating said, and they continued to walk.

At a shorter distance, Ginny could see that the man was, indeed, Smith, the porter, and he must have seen her approaching and attempted to hide, although not very well. Ginny quickened her pace.

"It's him," she told the detective, who began to walk swiftly alongside her, as fast as he could given his girth. Soon Hendrik joined their pace.

Smith ran out from behind the doorway and tried

to flee down the corridor when Detective Keating shouted at him.

"You, porter, stop right there!"

Smith continued his dash away from them until the detective yelled, "Stop immediately, sir, I am a detective!"

That caused Smith to stop in his tracks and face them. He panted.

"I'm sorry, I didn't know who you were or what you wanted," he said.

Ginny didn't believe him one bit.

"You know quite well who I am," she said when she and Detective Keating and Hendrik reached him.

"Do you know this woman?" Keating demanded from the man.

"I don't recognize her, no," he said.

Ginny gasped. "That isn't true."

"I think he's lying," Hendrik said to Keating.

"I am not, sir," Smith said to Hendrik.

"You know very well you saw me, Mr. Smith," Ginny told him. "I spoke to you outside my room while you were cleaning the windows. I asked you about a note I'd found, remember?"

Smith seemed to grasp he wouldn't get away with lying. "Right, I think I remember that. I didn't recognize you at first. I speak with a lot of passengers."

"I'm sure you do," Ginny said with a touch of sarcasm and pursed lips.

"What can I do for you, ma'am?" Smith asked her.

Ginny indicated to Detective Keating.

"Miss Weltermint," he said to her. "Is this the man you claim to have seen?"

"This is the man I *saw*," Ginny said.

"All right," Keating said and turned his attention to

Smith. "What you can do for me, sir, is produce a sample of your handwriting so that I may compare it to the one on this note." He held up the slip of paper for the porter to see.

Smith looked as though he might try to dash off again. "I had nothing to do with it," he said.

"Your answer was awfully fast," Hendrik remarked.

"Please, Mr. Bergen, this is a matter for the law to handle and not a civilian," Detective Keating told him, although he seemed to have become accustomed to their presence by then.

Hendrik nodded. "Of course. Pardon my intrusion."

"Did you leave the note in my room?" Ginny outright asked the porter.

The detective interrupted her. "Miss, this is my matter."

Ginny, too, nodded and then was quiet.

"As I said, sir, I would like a sample of your handwriting. Could you please write your name for me? Has anyone got any paper?"

Ginny offered a piece and a pencil she found in her purse.

Smith spoke to the detective. "Why do you need me to do this?"

"So that I can compare your writing to that of the note."

"I didn't write it," he said.

"A sample shall help clear your name quickly," Keating said matter-of-factly. He took the materials Ginny held out and passed them to Smith.

"I don't have anything to lean on," Smith complained.

"We shall go into the dining car, and you can write on one of the tables."

"It's closed," Smith said.

Ginny reasoned the porter's logic was that he didn't want to complete the task, and why was that?

"Can't we just go in for a moment? This will only take a moment," Keating said.

"No one is supposed to go in there at the moment," Smith replied.

"Only for a moment?"

"Not even for a moment."

Detective Keating sighed and frowned. "Well, then, lean against a wall or something of the sort. I do need you to write something for me."

It seemed the more Detective Keating pressed the matter, the more nervous the porter became, and the more Ginny felt he was hiding something.

"Is everything all right, Mr. Smith?" she asked him.

"Yes, ma'am. Why wouldn't it be?" was his reply.

"You seem quite nervous, actually," Ginny said, and Hendrik murmured in agreement.

"I am not," Smith said with some resentment. He looked at the detective. "I am not, I just don't know how I'm supposed to write my name if I haven't got a table to lean on."

Detective Keating handed Ginny's materials to him. "You can lean against the wall, sir. Please proceed."

Smith held the paper and pencil limply in his hands.

"Well?" Keating inquired. "Aren't you going to begin?"

The man sighed and fidgeted with the paper, and, again, Ginny wondered whether he would attempt to bolt away. He seemed very nervous, as if his handwriting could match the note.

"Sir?" Detective Keating demanded.

Smith dropped the materials at his feet. "Someone paid me to leave the note and turn on her record player, but I didn't write it," he suddenly said.

11

Ginny gasped and Hendrik had to steady her. Was she in the killer's sights?

Detective Keating looked at Smith carefully. "Who paid you, sir?"

"I can't say." Smith gulped.

"Why not?"

"I just can't. I'm sorry."

Ginny felt the porter seemed very frightened and wondered if the person who'd paid him had also threatened him.

"Do you know that I can arrest you for covering for this person once I find them?" Detective Keating spoke in frustration.

"Then you'll just have to do that, if you ever find them."

Detective Keating eyed him closely. "And why is that, sir?"

"Because I can't reveal who they are."

"They must have paid you very handsomely," Keating remarked.

"Indeed, sir."

Detective Keating gasped and looked shocked.

"You are admitting you are keeping quiet simply because you accepted a bribe? I am certainly within my rights to place you under arrest."

Smith remained quiet and still, and Ginny thought that he looked rather stoic. She waited for Detective Keating to put handcuffs on the porter.

Instead, Detective Keating continued to question the man. "Can you tell me something about this person, whether they are a lady or a gentleman, perhaps?" he asked him.

The porter shook his head. "I cannot, sir."

"What do you owe them that you cannot tell me?"

The man looked at the ground and wouldn't speak.

"I think he's frightened," Ginny spoke up. "Did whoever paid you to leave the note in my cabin threaten you?" she asked the porter.

Smith wouldn't say.

"Why did you play that song in particular?" Ginny asked.

Smith was quiet.

"I ought to arrest you," Detective Keating said to the man, again. "At the very least, I ought to get you fired for bothering Miss Weltermint."

"I didn't mean to alarm her," the man replied and apologized to Ginny.

Ginny would have felt rather odd accepting his apology, so she just nodded.

"The person who paid you could be connected to the murder, or might even be the culprit themselves," the detective said. "Can you tell me whether they are young or old?"

Smith remained looking at the ground as he shook his head.

Scripted Murder

"Oh," Detective Keating said to the man in frustration. "You aren't going to tell me anything at all, are you?"

Smith looked up and nodded.

"Outrageous," Detective Keating declared. After a moment, he said, "I will still need a handwriting sample from you."

"Why, if I didn't write the note?" Smith asked.

"Because you could be lying. How can I trust your word when you won't tell me who paid you to put the note in Miss Weltermint's room?"

The man seemed to comprehend his logic, and Ginny sensed he grasped that it was a situation he wouldn't get out of easily. He picked up the paper and pencil from the floor and held the paper against the wall. He wrote his name slowly as all three watched. He handed the paper to the detective, who took it and examined it in the light alongside the note he held in his hand.

"The handwriting isn't the same," Detective Keating declared after a few moments.

"See, I told you I was telling the truth," Smith said.

"That does not make you an honest man," Keating remarked.

"Can I go now, sir?" Smith asked him.

The detective thought for a moment. "Yes, you can be on your way."

Ginny looked at Keating. "You're just going to let him go?"

"I'll say. What's going on here?" Hendrik asked him.

As the porter walked away, the detective explained his reasoning to them.

"I'm not going to do anything at the moment. Even

if I simply go to his superiors about him, it is quite possible they will boot him off the train and Mr. Smith will never be seen again. And if I arrest him, I believe it is less likely I will find the killer. I feel it is more likely I will catch the killer with him loose. I believe he will trip up soon and lead me to the culprit, so for the time being, I want him around. As much as I wish I could, I cannot force the name out of him," he said with a slight smile. "I promise you I will keep an eye on him."

Both Ginny and Hendrik nodded at his logic, although for her part, she felt a bit more on edge with the porter about the place. Was the note writer the killer, and was the porter somehow involved in the murder, or was he lying and was himself the killer?

Hendrik seemed to sense her apprehension and asked her, "Are you all right?"

"I suppose I will be. I can't help but feel a little alarmed with him running about the place and knowing he put that note in my room."

"Yes, I do wonder if you should have arrested the porter," he said to Detective Keating.

"I can understand his reasoning," Ginny told Hendrik.

"Perhaps, darling, but, still, I do wonder."

Darling. The word startled her pleasantly. Ginny knew something good was happening between them, and so soon after Paul, but some things did happen that way; some things couldn't wait.

"Don't worry," Hendrik told her. "I'll make sure nothing happens to you." He gave her a sincere smile.

"And if it will offer you some comfort, miss, I will keep an eye on you as well," Detective Keating said to her.

His kind gesture surprised her, and she thanked both of them.

Detective Keating parted ways with the pair, and she and Hendrik discussed going to the lounge where a proper warm meal was to be served, as the kitchen had been reopened. They settled on going, and Ginny expressed interest in having Scarlet join them since the cat was permitted in the lounge. They walked together to Ginny's cabin and passed the Warwicks in the corridor. She and Hendrik said hello to both. Mrs. Warwick nodded and smiled slightly at them, while Mr. Warwick gave them a short nod, which wasn't bad considering, and at least he hadn't ignored her. Ginny knew not to expect much, but the upper-crust part of her didn't like anyone being upset with her, especially not her elders.

Hendrik insisted on going inside her room first, just in case, although after the note incident, she would never again forget to lock the door. Ginny could hear Scarlet mewing in the room.

"We're coming, darling," she spoke to the cat as she unlocked the door.

Hendrik slowly opened the door.

"You should wait out here. I'll go inside and take a look," he whispered to her, as though someone might be inside.

Ginny's heart raced as he gradually entered the room. At first, she doubted anyone was inside, but now that the door was open, she felt it might be possible. After all, the porters might have keys to the rooms, and that man Smith had admitted to going into her room before. Detective Keating had promised he'd watch out for her, but he was a very busy man at the moment.

Scarlet came to greet Ginny, peeking her head around the doorway, as Ginny waited just outside of it for Hendrik.

"Hello, you," Ginny said quietly to the cat and reached down to scratch her neck. Scarlet enjoyed the feeling and rubbed into her touch. Ginny listened for sounds that Hendrik might be in danger, and soon he appeared in the doorway.

"There's nothing to be afraid of," he announced.

"You don't know how grateful I am to hear that," Ginny said, exhaling.

He motioned for her to enter the room, and she stepped inside to get Scarlet's lead so that she could walk her around the train. Hendrik waited for her while she freshened up in her room, and Ginny slipped the lead on the cat. She and Hendrik exited her room, and she locked the door.

They went down the corridor toward the lounge and went by a group of passengers, two men and two women, who looked like they were couples. From what Ginny could overhear, they seemed to be discussing a plan to get off the train. Ginny asked Hendrik if he'd heard it also, and he nodded.

One of the men grabbed Ginny's arm as she walked past him, and Hendrik scolded him and removed his hand from Ginny.

"What do you think you're doing?" he demanded.

The man, in a dark suit, had red-rimmed eyes and seemed maddened. "I saw you with that detective in the lounge, both of you, so you must know what's going on. They eventually told us that someone was killed but wouldn't say more. When are they going to let us off this train? You must know something since you're chummy with that gumshoe."

"Calm down, Mr.—?"

"George, the name's George," the fellow said.

"George, you need to have a little more respect for the lady," Hendrik said.

The man apologized to Ginny.

"That's all right. This situation has gotten the best of many of us," she replied.

"It just feels like we'll be on this train forever," one of the women chimed in.

Ginny offered her sympathy.

"Can you tell us anything?" the other woman asked. "Are you friends with that man who looks like a detective?"

"I wouldn't exactly call us friends," Hendrik said.

"Yes, we've sort of attached ourselves to him despite his objections," Ginny said.

The women smiled at her humor, but both of the men seemed exasperated. Ginny wouldn't have been surprised if they intended to stage a mutiny.

"I'm afraid I don't know anything substantial," Ginny said. "But I can tell you he's still investigating the case," she added without giving too much away.

"Is he likely to solve it soon?" the other man asked her. "They told us we had to remain on board until they figured out which one of us is the murderer."

Ginny knew that Detective Keating would be most displeased if she revealed any of the pertinent facts of the case to these strangers, so she replied, "I'm afraid I really have no idea," before Hendrik could answer, as she didn't know if he would be as discreet as her.

"Are you in first class?" Hendrik asked the couples.

The women nodded.

"I heard they're going to serve a hot meal in the

lounge if you're interested. We're on our way there now."

Ginny reckoned it was his way of changing the course of the conversation, and she was grateful.

One of the women laughed at the sight of Scarlet on her leash. "A cat on a leash, and I thought I'd seen everything!" she exclaimed to Ginny. "She's like a little dog."

"And almost trained like one too," Ginny said to the woman.

"We'll probably go to the lounge, like you suggested," the woman said.

The men with them seemed a bit more reluctant, and the George fellow kept pressing them for information.

"Listen, fellow, you really can't tell me anything? Fellow to fellow? I promise you we'll keep it to ourselves," he said to Hendrik.

"I'm sorry, George, but I haven't got a clue," he replied, going along with Ginny.

"The detective didn't even give you a hint about when he's likely to finish?"

"I know probably just as much as you do," Hendrik said. "I'm afraid we haven't learned much."

"You must at least know a little more than we do," the other man said.

Hendrik sighed and seemed to be debating what to tell them, and Ginny hoped he wouldn't tell too much. She squeezed his arm.

"All I know," Hendrik spoke carefully as though he didn't want to panic the man, "is that he hasn't solved the case yet. He's still investigating."

"Yes, but do you know how close he is to finishing?" one of the women asked him.

If Ginny had thought they would stay out of it, she'd been wrong, and soon both couples were ganging up on her and Hendrik.

"I don't think it's very fair you have him at your disposal while the rest of us are kept in the dark," the other woman remarked.

Ginny introduced herself and shook the woman's hand. "Ginny Weltermint."

"She's a Weltermint, that's why he's talking to her!" the woman said to the group.

"Ginny hasn't gotten special treatment," Hendrik came to her defense. "She's still on board this train like everyone else."

"Yeah, but that detective fellow is always talking to her," one of the men said.

"I can assure you that it's the other way around," Ginny said calmly. "You can speak to him yourself if you'd like," she suggested.

"I have, and he's told me nothing," the man said.

"The only reason I got involved in the first place is because I found the body," Ginny said.

Both of the women gasped, and one of them backed away from Ginny as though she could have been the murderer.

"I didn't have anything to do with it," Ginny said with a laugh.

"Did you see it, too?" one of the men asked Hendrik.

He shook his head.

The revelation seemed to diffuse them, and they quieted. Ginny and Hendrik were able to continue to the lounge with the couples walking far behind them as if they were afraid of getting too close. Ginny imagined they wouldn't bother her for the remainder of the time.

"Shouldn't we tell Detective Keating about the plans we overheard those couples making?" she asked Hendrik.

"Do you think they're serious about it?"

"I'm not sure. Those men seemed awfully determined. Part of me feels like we're passengers too and shouldn't say anything, but I wouldn't want to see the detective's work jeopardized."

"I think you're too kind," Hendrik said with a smile. "You're being very considerate of the detective, who most likely won't be grateful. But that's one of the things I'm growing to like about you."

His words made her face fill with warmth, and she thanked him.

"But, sure, let's go find the detective and tell him," Hendrik said.

They went in search of Detective Keating, with Scarlet's nose leading the way. Hendrik pointed him out in the corridor ahead, speaking with one of his policemen.

"Detective Keating," Ginny said.

He looked at her with a "Now what?" expression on his face. He looked down at Scarlet, and Ginny thought she saw him smile for a second.

"There's something we think we should tell you," Ginny said.

"Something about the murder?"

"Not exactly," Hendrik said.

"Well, then?" The detective waited for one of them to explain.

"We thought you should know that we overheard a couple of the passengers discussing a...mutiny of sorts. They said they're planning to try to get off the train," Ginny said.

Detective Keating frowned. "And what are their names?"

"I'm afraid we didn't get all their names," Hendrik said. "One of the fellows is named George, but I don't know his last name."

The detective shook his head at them as if they should have known better. He looked around at the passengers moving about the corridor. "Can you point them out to me?"

Ginny searched but didn't see them. "I'm afraid I don't see them."

Hendrik craned his neck. "I don't either."

"And you don't know their names except that one of them is 'George'? Then of what use is this information to me?" The detective sounded exasperated.

"We just thought you should know," Ginny said. "There were two men and two women. The men seemed to be the ringleaders."

"Do you know how many 'two men' and 'two women' there must be on this train?" Detective Keating said.

"I know, there must be many," Ginny said.

"How do you expect me to find them?"

"If we see them again, we'll point them out," Hendrik said.

"Yes, well, I hope you can."

"We really just wanted to notify you so you could be on the lookout," Hendrik said.

"I'll station some more men at the exits to quell any unrest," Detective Keating said.

"We're on our way to the lounge. A hot meal is

supposed to be served," Ginny said. "Would you like to join us?"

"I think I've joined you enough for a while," Keating replied.

"Very well," Hendrik said and took Ginny's arm in his. They went toward the lounge.

12

Ginny and Hendrik had a quiet, pleasant meal in the lounge with the other first-class passengers. The rest of the passengers were served more coffee or tea and sandwiches in their seats or their rooms. Ginny looked for the Warwicks but didn't see them and wondered how Mrs. Warwick was faring and if her husband still resented Ginny for bringing Detective Keating into their room.

She kept an eye out for the couples in the lounge but didn't see them enter. Perhaps they had decided not to have a meal, or perhaps they had gathered somewhere else and were planning their mutiny.

She insisted on paying the check this time and was pleased to see Hendrik at ease with that. They moved into the smoking room, where some of the passengers had gathered to complain among themselves, and where Ginny, although she'd gotten over the confrontation with the couples in the corridor, still fretted about the earlier exchange with Mr. Warwick. She disliked being on anyone's bad side. Hendrik seemed to sense her concern.

"What's wrong, Ginny?" he asked.

She reached down to stroke Scarlet in her lap. She told Hendrik her anxiety about Mr. Warwick.

"A man Mr. Warwick's age is bound to have a thick skin," Hendrik told her. "I should think he will forget about it very soon, if he is even still upset. He is a unique man, much like our detective, and tricky to read, so I wouldn't assume he's still upset over the matter. One can't really be sure what's going on in his head."

His words gave Ginny some comfort, but she still fretted.

"I can't stand having someone dislike me," Ginny admitted to Hendrik.

"So many of us feel that way," he replied with a sympathetic smile. "But we just have to carry on as before and hope they get over it eventually. Mr. Warwick seems like a sensible man, and I don't think he's the type to hold a grudge for long. Besides, you'll probably never see him again after this ordeal."

"True," Ginny said. "Yet one never knows who one might come across in one's social circle." Truthfully, she couldn't stand the thought of someone out there who resented her. Ginny stroked Scarlet in her lap, and she and Hendrik finished their meal.

The couples who had confronted them in the corridor entered the smoking room and sat down and seemed to be discussing something. But what? Their mutiny? Ginny moved to her right so that they couldn't see her behind Hendrik, who sat with his back to them, and pointed out their presence to him.

"They're directly behind you," Ginny said. "Which one of us should run to tell Detective Keating? I wouldn't want them to think we tattled on them to the detective. I would go myself, but I'm a bit afraid to walk past their table because they're more likely to recognize me."

"I'll go," Hendrik offered.

He quietly left the table, walking around the couples' table rather than towards it. Ginny moved farther to the right, but it was no use, for one of the women looked straight at her and pointed her out to the others, and they each gave her a little wave. Ginny had no choice but to acknowledge them with a half-smile. She wondered whether they'd ask her to join them now that they'd cooled down a bit. They didn't seem as taken aback by her connection to the murder as before, and she could see they were intrigued by her. Perhaps they wanted to ask her questions about her discovery of the body. Once Keating arrived, they would surely make the connection between Ginny being there and him questioning them. That made her on the detective's side, whether he liked it or not.

Just as Hendrik entered the room with Detective Keating, one of the women got up to invite her to their table. Then she saw the detective marching towards her and retreated. Hendrik returned to Ginny's side.

"I do feel guilty we told on them because I can understand where they're coming from," she told him.

"Don't fret," he said. "We did the right thing." He reached across the table to squeeze her hand. Scarlet hissed at him, as though the feline resented his attachment to her owner.

Out of the corner of her eye, Ginny watched the detective speaking with the couples. He seemed to be asking them to step outside the lounge. Would he arrest them?

The couples reluctantly rose from their seats and

followed him. As they were being escorted away, one of the women stopped at Ginny's table.

"Tattlers," she hissed. "I know it was you who told him. You overheard us."

"I have no idea what you're talking about," Hendrik answered, but Ginny kept quiet.

She could see the detective speaking with them outside the doorway, and he seemed to have put them in their place, for they strode away looking defeated.

"I think the mutiny is over," Ginny informed Hendrik, who couldn't see the interaction. "What do you say we call it a night?"

Hendrik agreed, and as they left the lounge, Ginny noticed more men stationed at the exits and imagined no mutiny could ever occur.

She and Hendrik retreated to their cabins for the night. When morning came, Ginny saw the sun peeking in through the curtain in her room. She sat up in bed and stroked Scarlet's soft coat. There had been an announcement made the evening before in the lounge about breakfast being offered at no charge the next morning. She and Hendrik had agreed to meet at the lounge to dine together. Ginny washed and dressed and changed Scarlet's newspapers and gave her fresh water and food. Ginny hoped to run into Detective Keating at breakfast to ask him for an update on his investigation, but she had to be careful not to seem too eager.

Scarlet yawned and extended her front paws, claws out, in a restful stretch before relaxing into a ball of fur. Ginny left her on the bed and went out into the corridor and locked the door behind her. She went toward the lounge and half-wondered whether she'd see the Warwicks since she always seemed to run into them, but she didn't. She reached the lounge and found Hendrik waiting outside the doorway for her. He had a newspaper tucked under his arm.

"Good morning," he said to her with a grin.

"Good morning," she said.

"They delivered some updated newspapers to us this morning. I see our train has made the front page." He said, unfolding it and showing it to her.

Ginny read the headline.

Murder Halts Express Train!

It was a regional paper and wouldn't have contained anything about her and Paul, for which Ginny was thankful.

"They've all descended upon us," Hendrik said. "Take a look out the window." He gestured to the window behind them.

Ginny looked. About a dozen newspapermen waited outside with cameras, and some were photographing the train. Ginny ducked at the sight of a flashbulb.

"Is everything all right?" Hendrik asked.

She reminded him who she was and about Paul.

"Oh, right," he said, helping her away. "Let's get you inside the lounge."

Ginny crouched as she walked until she realized some of the other passengers were staring at her and she was drawing attention to herself. Perhaps she had looked ill or mad.

Most of the tables were occupied, but Hendrik managed to find a table near the back of the car. The smell of the food hit her as soon as she entered, and she realized how hungry she was.

"Thank you for rescuing me," Ginny said.

"It was my pleasure."

The breakfast was set up buffet style, and Hendrik offered to fill a plate for her. "I assume you want all the usual breakfast?" he asked her.

"Oh, yes, that would be very nice, thank you."

"I'll also get us some coffee," he said.

Ginny had smelled a strong brew upon their arrival.

Their table was far removed from the window, tucked behind two other tables, so it was unlikely anyone would be able to see in from outside, but Ginny still crouched a little in her seat. She expected to see the Warwicks there, but didn't, and she wondered how Mrs. Warwick was feeling. A few tables in front of her were the mutiny couples, and one of the women glowered at her. Ginny shrugged. She hadn't thought about it before, but now she wondered how the couples knew one another and if they were traveling for vacation. As for their annoyance with her for ruining their plans, she and Hendrik had helped the detective and prevented a potential disruption in the flow of his investigation, for if four passengers left, who knew how many might follow? And although it hadn't made her any new friends, she felt she had acted properly.

Hendrik returned to the table with two plates of food and cups of coffee. There were a few waiters circling about, but not enough to help him bring it over. He set her plate and coffee in front of her, and Ginny thanked him.

He sat across from her. "Forgive me if I don't do much talking. I'm quite hungry." He grinned.

"I'm rather famished too," Ginny said. "So I don't mind." She sipped her coffee, which tasted wonderfully warm and robust. "I do hope they won't allow those newspapermen aboard."

"I doubt it. Detective Keating doesn't want anyone coming on or going off unless they're with the police..."

A man in a suit approached their table from the side, and Ginny didn't recognize him. For some reason, he had his hand behind his back.

He smiled at her, and she could see he had very narrow teeth. "Excuse me, miss, are you Virginia Weltermint?" he asked her.

Ginny didn't know how to react. She didn't believe she knew the man, but she'd met so many people throughout her life that she couldn't be sure. Perhaps he knew her family. Or he recognized her from the newspapers. Just in case she had met him or he knew her family, she smiled cordially and said lightly, "Yes, I am. But I'm afraid I don't know who you are. Have we met somewhere?"

"Max Port," he said, shaking her hand. "One of the policemen stationed outside told me you found the body, and I recognized your name. I'm with the *Times*." He moved his hand out from behind himself, and she saw that he had a camera.

Ginny let go of his hand. "You're a newspaperman?"

The man tried to take her picture as Hendrik rose and blocked him. "Leave the lady alone," he said sharply. "How did you get on the train?"

"I sneaked on. Let me take just one picture." He attempted to maneuver around Hendrik.

"You'll do no such thing," Hendrik said. "You'll leave now."

A few of the other passengers watched their interaction.

The newsman seemed determined to photograph her. "Just one picture, miss." Once more, he tried to sneak around Hendrik's large frame.

It became clear the man would not leave, and Hendrik grabbed Ginny's hand and pulled her up from the table.

"Come on," he said to her. "I say we should run."

They raced out of the smoking room together with the newspaperman trailing after them. Outside in the corridor, Detective Keating shouted, "What in heaven's name is going on?" He noticed the man with the camera chasing after them and ordered all of them to stop running.

Hendrik spoke over his shoulder, "Only if he agrees to not take Ginny's picture."

Detective Keating jogged up to the man and grabbed the camera from him, and Hendrik and Ginny halted.

"Give me back my camera," the newsman said to him.

"How did you get on this train?" Detective Keating demanded. "You aren't supposed to be on here, sir."

"I sneaked past when one of your policemen wasn't paying attention."

"I order you to leave at once. You are interfering with my investigation." The detective looked in Ginny's direction, and she realized he'd asked the man to leave for her sake.

"I wouldn't have come on board in the first place if one of your policemen hadn't told me that a Weltermint found the body," the man said.

"One of my policemen told you this?" Detective Keating eyed with him carefully.

"He certainly did."

A policeman who had been stationed in the distance started walking towards them, and Detective Keating motioned to him. "Please escort this...gentleman outside."

The policeman nodded and motioned for the man to follow him.

"My camera," the man said to Keating.

Detective Keating removed the film so he couldn't photograph Ginny on his way out and pocketed it before handing the camera back to him. Still, Ginny imagined there would be a write-up in the gossip columns at some point: *Paul Blair's Former Flame Finds Body and New Romance!*

"What about my film?" the man asked Keating.

"You'll have to do without it," the detective replied, and Ginny grinned to herself.

The policeman took the newspaperman away, and Detective Keating said to Ginny, "You have my word, miss, that whichever of my policemen disclosed to that newsman that it was you who found the body will be personally reprimanded by me."

Ginny started to thank him when the detective was called away by another policeman. Ginny heard a few words of their conversation, and said to Hendrik, "Another passenger has been murdered."

13

HENDRIK HAD TO MAKE AN IMPORTANT BUSINESS CALL, but Ginny followed Detective Keating and the policeman to the vicinity of where the first body had been discovered.

Mr. Warwick stood in the corridor by an open room with another policeman at his side.

"Mr. Warwick, what are you doing here?" Ginny asked him.

Detective Keating ordered the policeman standing with Mr. Warwick to block off the corridor and entered the room himself.

"I discovered the body," Mr. Warwick said to Ginny. He no longer seemed upset about the note incident. Either that or he was too distracted to remember it.

"Did you see who it is?" Ginny asked him.

"His name's Mr. Oliver Doyle. He's a first-class passenger like us. I discovered him deceased. I was on my way to get a cup of tea for myself and Mrs. Warwick – she is still feeling ill – and I knocked on Mr. Doyle's door because he and I were acquainted, to see if he wanted a cup of tea also. I found his door ajar and him on the floor inside."

"How dreadful," Ginny said. She could see the corpse, in a suit, crumpled on the floor.

Another policeman arrived and entered the room and spoke with Detective Keating. From what she overheard, it seemed Mr. Doyle had been strangled with something like a wire. A tidy murder compared to the first, and Ginny wondered if the killer was the same. Ginny waited with Mr. Warwick in the corridor while Detective Keating worked inside the room with the other policeman.

After a while, Detective Keating emerged from the room alone to speak with Mr. Warwick.

"Do you mind, miss?" he asked Ginny, as though he wanted her to step away.

"I don't mind if she stays," Mr. Warwick said.

"Yes, but..."

"I could stay here to support Mr. Warwick," Ginny suggested.

"Yes, I would like that," Mr. Warwick said.

Detective Keating cleared his throat as though he was a bit annoyed. "There does seem to be quite a lot of supporting happening on this train," he murmured.

"What can I say, we're a very supportive bunch," Ginny said.

Detective Keating seemed determined to leave her out of the matter and spoke to Mr. Warwick with his back to Ginny.

Mr. Warwick told the detective the same thing that he'd told Ginny.

"And did you see anyone else in the vicinity when you discovered the body?" the detective asked him.

"Do you mean, did I see anyone suspicious?" Mr. Warwick replied.

"Yes, that."

"I did not, sir. I didn't see anyone in the corridor at the time. When I found Mr. Doyle, I immediately went to fetch one of your policemen."

"And did you move anything in the crime scene?" Detective Keating asked him.

"I most certainly did not. I didn't even enter the room all the way. I didn't check to see if Mr. Doyle was still alive because it was quite clear to me he was not. I called his name, but he didn't move, not once, and he didn't seem to be breathing."

"You are quite correct, sir. He appears to have been dead for many hours."

"He certainly looked like it," Mr. Warwick said.

"How well did you know Mr. Doyle?" Detective Keating asked him slowly. "Did you know him before the trip?"

Just what was Detective Keating getting at? Did he suspect Mr. Warwick?

"Not very well. We became acquainted on the train," Mr. Warwick told the detective as Ginny waited and listened. "I do hope you're not implying I could have something to do with this monstrosity."

"I am a detective, sir, so I have to consider all possibilities, unfortunately."

Mr. Warwick breathed out as though in disgust and shook his head. "I can assure you that I had nothing to do with this poor man's demise. I simply wanted to know if he would have appreciated a cup of tea. You don't know me well, sir, but I can tell you that I am an honest man."

Ginny felt that Mr. Warwick's words sounded truthful and interjected on his behalf.

"I do believe he's telling the truth," she said, tapping the detective's back.

He eyed her over his shoulder. "I will determine that," he replied.

"It's the truth," Mr. Warwick insisted. "There is nothing to determine. I am telling you the truth."

Detective Keating didn't say anything. Instead, he turned from Mr. Warwick and looked at Ginny. "Did you know Mr. Doyle?" he asked her.

She shook her head.

"I had to check," the detective said. He turned to Mr. Warwick. "And as far as you go, Mr. Warwick, I shall see."

"I don't very much like what you're getting at," Mr. Warwick said. "My wife can tell you that I left my room only a little while ago, and so, I couldn't have killed this man," he spoke with impunity.

"I think I shall do just that," Detective Keating said and trotted off to the Warwicks' room down the corridor.

Ginny and Mr. Warwick followed him.

"I do hope this nonsense is cleared up soon," Mr. Warwick spoke to Ginny as they walked.

"I'm sure it will be over very soon," Ginny replied. "I am sorry about before."

"Oh, that's all right, dear, I've forgotten all about it." Mr. Warwick smiled in a genuine way.

At the Warwicks' cabin, Detective Keating gestured for Mr. Warwick to open the door, probably so not to barge in on Mrs. Warwick. Mr. Warwick opened the door, and Detective Keating and Ginny followed him inside the room.

Mrs. Warwick was sitting up in the bed in her dressing gown, reading. "What are all these people doing in my room again?" she asked her husband.

"Another crime has been committed," Detective Keating stated.

Mrs. Warwick gasped and dropped her book to the bed. "How dreadful. Are you all right, dear?" she asked her husband.

"Yes, dear. It was Mr. Doyle. I'm afraid I found him dead," Mr. Warwick told his wife.

"Oh, how awful," Mrs. Warwick exclaimed. She looked at Ginny. "What do you have to do with what's happened, dear girl?"

"Miss Weltermint has been kind enough to accompany me for support," Mr. Warwick said, and Ginny could see that all was good between them.

"How unfortunate for Mr. Doyle," Mrs. Warwick said. "He seemed like such a pleasant man."

"How well did you know Mr. Doyle?" Detective Keating asked her. "Your husband mentioned he didn't know him well."

"I beg your pardon, sir," Mr. Warwick said. "Are you implying that my wife and Mr. Doyle were... friends behind my back?"

"Not at all, sir. I am merely trying to assess whether your wife has anything crucial to share with me."

"I knew him even less than my husband, I'm sure," Mrs. Warwick told the detective.

"Are you sure?" Detective Keating asked her skeptically.

Mrs. Warwick seemed appalled at his suggestion. "Absolutely," she said.

"Your husband has told me that he left this room

only a little while ago. Can you confirm this?" the detective asked Mrs. Warwick.

She nodded. "Yes, he left to get us some tea."

"And he never left the room prior to that?" Detective Keating questioned.

"No, he was with me the whole time before that."

"Very good," the detective said.

"I'm glad we have sorted this whole business out," Mr. Warwick said with an air of victory. "As you can see, I am innocent in Mr. Doyle's death."

"Yes, I can see that," the detective said. "My questioning you is nothing personal, sir, I can assure you, but a matter of routine. Now, are you very sure you didn't see anyone in the area of the room you discovered Mr. Doyle in? Or did you hear something, perhaps?" Detective Keating removed his notepad, as though he hoped to write something down.

"No, there was no one and nothing," Mr. Warwick answered him. "As far as I could tell, I was alone in the corridor, and there might have been the sounds of other passengers in the rooms and down the corridor, but nothing alarming."

"Very well," Detective Keating said. "That is all. If I have any other questions, I will find you."

"Fine, but I don't see what other questions you could possibly have."

"Something unexpected might turn up," the detective replied.

Mr. Warwick glowered at him.

"Did you manage to get us any tea, dear?" Mrs. Warwick asked her husband.

"I'm afraid not, dear. I shall get us some momentarily." Mr. Warwick turned to the detective again.

"Have we finished? I'd like to get my wife some tea now."

Detective Keating nodded. "Good day, Mr. and Mrs. Warwick."

"Yes, certainly, I shall have a good day now that we are through with this business," Mr. Warwick said with a scowl.

Ginny quietly said goodbye to the Warwicks and followed Detective Keating out of the room.

"Are you still following me?" Detective Keating spoke over his shoulder as he walked.

"I am," Ginny said.

"Where's your companion?"

"Do you mean Hendrik? He had to make a telephone call."

"Don't you have better things to do, Miss Weltermint, than follow me around all day?"

"Perhaps, but this is more interesting. Otherwise, I'd just be waiting around like the other passengers. I hope you don't mind."

"I do, but I don't believe you'll listen."

Ginny trailed Detective Keating as he walked down the corridor and stopped when he entered the deceased's room again, past the policemen standing guard.

"Goodbye, Miss Weltermint," the detective spoke to her as though he wanted her to go away.

"Goodbye, detective," she said.

But she didn't leave. She waited outside the doorway, pretending to be going through her purse, and saw Detective Keating dusting the room for fingerprints. Ginny overheard him telling the policeman inside that the man had been killed some time in the middle of the night, and that nothing appeared to be missing from the deceased's room, but, like the first crime scene, the murder had been done very neatly and there were no fingerprints.

"This second murder wouldn't have happened if everyone had obeyed my original rule and stayed put," Detective Keating complained to the policeman.

"Yes, sir, but you couldn't have expected them to do so for very long," the policeman replied.

"Yes, but still, people simply don't know how to behave themselves these days," the detective griped.

When Detective Keating exited the room, Ginny stopped him.

"What are you still doing here?" he asked her. "I thought you left. Have you been here the whole time?"

"I'm still here all right," Ginny said. "Could the two murders be connected?" she asked him.

Detective Keating seemed to debate whether he should tell her. He seemed somewhat flattered by her interest, and she remembered his work didn't intrigue his wife or daughters. "From the outset, these two men don't appear to be connected," he said after a moment. "There is something odd, though."

"What is it?"

The detective paused and seemed to be considering whether he should tell her. Perhaps he thought she would leave if he didn't reply to her. He must not have known Ginny very well, however, because she stayed put.

"Mr. Doyle, the second victim, spoke to me earlier and told me there was something he wanted to discuss with me," Keating said when he saw she wasn't going anywhere, and perhaps he wanted someone to vent to regardless. "We'd arranged to meet later, but never got the chance to, obviously."

"Perhaps that means he either suspected or knew the identity of the first killer and was killed because of that," Ginny said.

Detective Keating nodded. "Yes, I believe so, miss."

Mr. Warwick had been cleared. That left the porter Smith, Maureen Vix, and herself.

"You can't possibly assume any longer that Maureen Vix or I had something to do with both of these deaths?" Ginny asked Detective Keating.

"We shall see, madam," he replied.

"Does that mean I'm still under suspicion?"

He nodded. "Mr. Doyle most likely was killed sometime in the night or very early this morning. What were you doing during this time?"

"I was asleep in my room," Ginny replied.

"Was anyone with you?" he asked delicately, as though he meant Hendrik.

She put her hand to her chest and acted shocked. "Detective, I'm surprised at your impudence. Of course I was alone." Although the idea had crossed her mind.

"I do apologize, miss, but I do have to ask these sorts of...unfortunate questions sometimes. I do know you are a lady, miss. I don't doubt that."

"Yes, I am a lady," she spoke with mock outrage, enjoying his flattery.

"I am sorry, miss." His eyes were downcast for a moment. Then he looked at her and returned to being the serious detective. "So, you have no one who can vouch for your whereabouts?"

"Only my cat. I really don't understand why you insist I could be involved in these murders. To me, it seems outrageous. I didn't even know these gentlemen."

"I've seen all sorts of things as a detective," Detective Keating said. "And people have all sorts of reasons for committing crimes."

"Yes, well, I didn't commit a crime, let alone two of them."

Hendrik appeared at the other end of the corridor, and Ginny waved to him. He seemed to be trying to get past the policeman blocking the entrance. Ginny gestured to Detective Keating.

"Hendrik's here, tell that policeman to let him through."

"Why should I do that?" Keating replied. "Mr. Bergen has no justifiable reason to be here, and neither do you, for that matter."

"Aren't you questioning me? Hendrik knows I'm being honest. Maybe you'll listen to him."

"How does he know that if he wasn't with you?" he asked.

"Yes, but he can attest to my character, to how I seemed when he left me last night, after dinner, that is," she spoke pointedly.

"All right," Detective Keating said, and he gestured to the policeman to let Hendrik pass through.

Hendrik said when he approached them, "The train's abuzz with stories. Everyone wants to know what's going on."

"I will make an announcement once everything is settled," Detective Keating replied. "The last thing I need is everyone panicking."

"Another man was murdered," Ginny told Hendrik.

His eyes widened. "Any connection to the first?"

"The detective doesn't believe the two men were connected," Ginny told him. "But he also told me something very interesting about something the second man had said to him."

"What was it?" Hendrik asked.

Ginny told him.

"That is interesting, indeed," Hendrik said. "It seems likely that was the reason he was killed."

Detective Keating nodded. "Yes, I do wish I had spoken with him sooner."

"I hope you didn't discover the body again," Hendrik said to Ginny.

"No, it was Mr. Warwick this time."

"The poor fellow. Is he all right? He seems like a tough man, though."

"He seemed all right when I last saw him, albeit a bit disturbed. He's with his wife now. The detective here was just questioning my whereabouts late last night and earlier today." Ginny gestured at Keating. "I told him you could attest to my character."

"Ginny's done nothing wrong, I'm sure of it," Hendrik stated to the detective.

"Yes, but can you provide an alibi for her? Miss Weltermint has told me she was alone during those times."

"I wasn't with her, no, but I just know she couldn't have been involved in any of this." Hendrik indicated to the deceased's room. "I was with her this morning, and she seemed fine. She couldn't have committed a crime beforehand. Her demeanor was ordinary."

"Yes, well, what someone is capable of would surprise you," the detective reiterated. "I also have to consider the fact that you could be compromised since, obviously, you have feelings for Miss Weltermint," he told Hendrik.

"Compromised? That's nonsense. I'm speaking the truth, detective."

"Did you know the deceased, a Mr. Oliver Doyle?" Detective Keating asked Hendrik.

"I've never met him. What did he do for a living?"

"He was a businessman."

"No, I'm not familiar with him."

"Very well, Mr. Bergen. Now, if you two would excuse me, I have work to do." Detective Keating looked at Ginny one last time. "I've cleared the Warwicks, but you, Miss Weltermint, and Miss Vix, and Mr. Smith, are still under suspicion." He retreated into Mr. Doyle's room.

Hendrik turned to her. "Are you all right, Ginny?"

"I will be, once I've cleared this up," she answered honestly. "I'm going to speak with Maureen and the porter myself. I'm not going to wait for Detective Keating to do it. Are you coming with me?" She started to walk down the corridor.

"I don't know if that's wise," Hendrik said. "I wouldn't want to intrude on the detective's investigation. He'll probably be very sour if we do."

"That never seemed to bother you before," Ginny said in surprise.

"Another murder's been committed. It somehow seems different now and more severe."

"All right," Ginny said, a little disappointed.

"Shall we meet up later?" Hendrik asked her.

"Yes, I'd like that."

"Good luck, Ginny."

14

Ginny went toward second class in search of Maureen and found her in the corridor with Cecilia, staring out the window at the crowd of newspapermen.

"I hope they take my picture," Cecilia said to Maureen with bright eyes. "I'd love to be in the papers. Maybe they'll take your picture, too, it could help your acting career," she told Maureen.

"My mother would just die," Maureen giggled.

"Hello, Maureen," Ginny said.

Maureen turned to look at her. "Oh, miss—Ginny. We heard that something else has happened!"

"Yes, I'm afraid it has."

"I wonder if the newspapermen outside have heard," Maureen said.

"Probably not yet," Ginny said. "The detective's going to be making an announcement later, but I can tell you that another crime has been committed."

"That's terrible," Maureen and Cecilia both said at the same time.

"May I have a word with you alone?" Ginny said to Maureen delicately.

Maureen suddenly looked worried. "Sure, miss." She told Cecilia she'd meet up with her later, and Cecilia continued down the corridor. "We got bored in the room and so were just taking a walk," Maureen said to Ginny.

"That sounds nice," Ginny said. "Is there anyone in your room?"

Maureen nodded. "The other two girls are in there resting."

Ginny looked around for a quiet place to talk with the girl and spotted an unoccupied corner that had a seat for one of the crewmen. She gestured to it. "Let's step over there, shall we?"

Maureen nodded and followed her.

"What do you need to talk with me about? Is everything all right with you?" Maureen asked her. "Did something happen to Mr. Bergen?" Her eyes widened.

Ginny patted her shoulder to calm her. "No, he's fine, darling." She paused and thought about the right way to approach the girl. "Maureen, if there's something you'd like to tell me," she said in a motherly way, "I'm here to listen." She smiled to appear approachable.

"I don't understand, ma'am," Maureen said, and Ginny saw how the girl became more formal under stress.

"Something about what's happened, perhaps?" Ginny suggested carefully. "Another man was murdered," she said when it was clear the girl wasn't understanding what she meant.

"My Lord, that's awful," Maureen said and put her hand to her mouth.

"It is very unfortunate." She paused. "Is there... anything you'd like to share?"

"I don't understand what you mean, ma'am—Miss Ginny."

"About what's happened?" Ginny hinted.

The revelation seemed to dawn on Maureen and her face paled. "Do you mean, do I know anything about what's happened?" she said softly.

Ginny nodded and braced for Maureen's response, whatever it would be.

Maureen looked confused. "Why would I know that, ma'am?" Another look of comprehension washed over her face. "Oh, you think I might have done it." Her gaze darkened. "Why are you accusing me? I thought we were friends, and that you were going to help me become an actress. I thought you were a nice lady."

Ginny now saw that the girl wasn't going to handle this questioning well, which wasn't so surprising given her age, but Ginny had assumed she would be more timid and wasn't prepared for such confidence.

"I still am going to help you, Maureen," Ginny said. "I've already got you an audition with my friend. And I consider you a friend."

"Pardon me, miss, but you don't sound like you're my friend."

"I'm sorry you're taking this the wrong way, Maureen. I didn't mean for it to come out like this. I just wanted to talk with you and let you know I'm here for you."

"Shouldn't that policeman be asking me these kinds of questions?" the girl replied, smarter than Ginny had assumed.

"Yes, but I thought that perhaps you'd be more at ease with me."

"So that you could then tell on me to him?"

"No, Maureen, that's not it..."

"I didn't do anything wrong," the girl said quickly.

Ginny nodded, but continued with her questions anyway. "The second man to die, his name was Oliver Doyle, did you know him?"

"Don't you mean, did he offer to take me to dinner as well? I don't know what kind of woman you think I am. If my mother heard you, she'd..."

"I think you're a lovely young woman, Maureen," Ginny said with sincerity. She asked slowly, "Was anyone with you last night or early this morning?"

"I was alone in my room for part of the night, but the other girls slept there last night, and they were there this morning also," Maureen said.

So, she didn't have an alibi for some of the previous night.

"Can anyone verify that you were in your room?" Ginny asked her.

Maureen shook her head. "You'll just have to take my word for it. I'd like to join Cecilia now, if that's all right."

"Yes, go on. Thank you, Maureen."

The girl nodded curtly and went on her way.

Ginny disliked what had transpired between Maureen and herself, but at least she had a few more answers. She did hope that Maureen, if innocent, would forgive her before they reached California. Next, Ginny went in search of the porter Smith. She came across another porter in the corridor and inquired if the man knew Smith's whereabouts. He pointed in the opposite direction.

"I last saw him down there," the man said, and so Ginny went that way.

She spotted Smith standing at one of the windows, looking out at the newsmen below, as Maureen and Cecilia had been doing before. Ginny imagined that many people found the press exciting, when she herself somewhat feared them.

"Did you see how many of them are out there?" Smith remarked to her, as though she were simply a passerby and he was unaware who she was.

"Yes, I see," Ginny replied to him. "One of them got on the train earlier."

Smith looked right at her when he recognized her voice.

"Oh, it's you," he said, and he seemed a bit off.

Ginny smelled booze on his breath. Ginny drank on occasion despite the ban, but if he had been the conductor instead of a porter, she would have gone straight to the detective about such behavior.

"What can I do for you, ma'am?" Smith grinned at her.

"Don't you think it would be better if you at least tried to mask your vices, Mr. Smith?" she said.

"Nobody's noticed except for you. My supervisors are too busy with everything that's been going on. I heard that something else happened. Was it another murder?" He gave her another drunken smile.

"I'm not at liberty to say."

"So, you do know. It pays to be cozy with that detective, now doesn't it?"

"Detective Keating and I are not acquaintances and certainly not friends, Mr. Smith. He also considers me a suspect."

"Also? So, I'm a suspect, too, like I thought. Who

would have thought, me and an upper-class lady like you having something in common? What are you always doing around him, then? You and that German fellow."

"Hendrik's Dutch," Ginny said.

"German, Dutch, same thing," Smith replied.

Ginny ignored his question. "The second man to be killed, his name is Oliver Doyle," she said. "Did you know him?"

"Was he in first class?"

"Yes, he was. How did you know that?"

"I just guessed. Otherwise, why would they bother, right?" He gave her a wink. "No, I don't know him. There are so many of you, it isn't easy to keep track."

Ginny didn't care for Mr. Smith but felt that he was being truthful.

"Where were you last night and early this morning, Mr. Smith?" she asked him regardless.

"Are you working for the detective, now?"

Ginny disregarded his comment and asked the question again.

"Last night? I was in the porter's car, sleeping," he answered.

"Was anyone else there with you?" Ginny asked.

"No, the other fellows were working."

"So, you were alone?"

"That's right."

"What about early this morning?" she asked.

"Earlier? I got up and felt like having a drink, so I had one. Then I went outside while it was still dark and stood by the railing and spoke to those newspaper fellows down below."

Smith seemed like a boastful fellow, and Ginny considered that the man might have been giving them information about what was occurring on the train.

"Go ask them, they can tell you where I was," Smith said, as though he knew she never would do that.

Ginny was quiet.

"Yeah, that's what I thought," Smith said. "One of the other porters told me he saw a fellow chasing you with a camera. You must have something to hide, miss. A big story, perhaps?" He spoke as though he knew her secret. "Why did that fellow with the camera want your picture so badly, huh? Are you famous? I heard you were related to some actors."

Had he given her name to the newspaperman Max Port and not a policeman like Mr. Port had said? Ginny wouldn't have put it past him.

"Goodbye, Mr. Smith," she said, not caring to speak with him further.

Smith didn't say anything and resumed looking out the window. Ginny walked down the corridor and went toward the second victim's room, where she looked past the guard and saw Detective Keating conferring with one of his policemen as the body was being taken away on a stretcher through the corridor. They would have to walk past the aisles to exit the train. If the other passengers had been in the dark about what exactly had transpired, they would soon realize what had happened.

Detective Keating went on his way opposite her, presumably to question Maureen and the porter about their alibis. Would either or both mention she had spoken to them?

Ginny went in search of Hendrik and knocked on his door, but he wasn't in his room. Perhaps he was making a business telephone call. She looked for him a little while longer but was unsuccessful. She contemplated going to the lounge by herself but was leery to go there alone after what had happened with that Max Port fellow. After about a half hour, she saw passengers gathering in the sitting area and Detective Keating, who must have returned from questioning Maureen and the porter, standing at the front of the aisle. Ginny went over and found a place to stand. She didn't see Hendrik anywhere.

Detective Keating motioned for everyone to settle, and after a few moments the car quieted.

"Ladies and gentlemen, I appreciate your cooperation during this time, and unfortunately, the train will be delayed for a bit longer as another crime has been committed."

Many passengers sighed and complained among themselves. Some were saying that they had seen another body being carried through the train earlier.

"How much longer is this going to take?" one man shouted. "We've already been stuck here for days."

Detective Keating tried to calm the crowd. "Sir, it will take some more time. But no more time than is needed."

"That doesn't answer my question," the man replied.

The detective ignored him.

A woman asked, "Are we in danger?"

Some of the passengers gasped and started to speculate among themselves. Detective Keating seemed as though he didn't want to disclose too much but had little choice since there had been witnesses to the transportation of the corpse.

"There has been a second death, yes," he stated calmly.

"Was it murder?" a man demanded.

Ginny knew the answer but kept quiet and waited for the detective to speak. He nodded, and the crowd gasped and one of the women started sobbing, and the woman seated beside her comforted her.

"One of us could be next!" a man exclaimed.

"Now, sir, please calm down," Detective Keating said.

"The killings – were they connected?" a thin man asked.

"I am not at liberty to say."

At that, the crowd grew restless and people began to rise from their seats and approach the detective, demanding answers.

"Do you have any idea who the murderer is?" a man shouted. "It must be one of us!"

"We're not safe here, are we?" a woman asked.

The policemen directly to Keating's left and right tried to make sure no one crowded him in, but Ginny debated whether she should intervene as the policemen barely seemed to be able to control the crowd.

She decided she must. "Now, now," Ginny said loudly and stepped in front of the detective, blocking the crowd from moving closer. "Detective Keating is doing all he can to move this along. It isn't his fault that we are all delayed here. And he doesn't have any more answers for you at this time. But you won't be in danger if everyone sticks together and looks out for one another."

"How can you be so sure we aren't in danger?" an elderly woman asked her.

Scripted Murder

"If we look out for one another and keep a close eye on things, I am sure we'll be fine," Ginny replied.

"You don't know that," a man said.

"Who are you, anyway, lady?" another man asked.

Although she was reluctant to, she decided to use her clout to help the detective because she knew it could get the other passengers to listen to him. "I'm Virginia Weltermint," she said.

"Are you related to the Weltermints?" a woman asked her.

Ginny nodded. "They're my parents," she said.

"She's a Weltermint," another woman exclaimed to the other passengers.

"Can I have your autograph? You aren't your parents but it's the second-best thing," a young man said to her.

Ginny nodded and took out a pencil from her purse and signed the magazine he'd thrust at her. A few other people asked her for her autograph, and she obliged.

"I think it would be best if everyone returned to their places to let the detective carry on with his work," Ginny said to the group afterwards.

Gradually, the crowd dispersed. Detective Keating turned to her in silence.

"Yes, detective?" she asked.

"Thank you, miss," he murmured.

"You're very welcome," Ginny replied. "Being a Weltermint does come in handy sometimes," she said with a wink.

"Yes, I can see it does."

Ginny asked, "Have you seen Mr. Bergen around anywhere? I was supposed to meet up with him."

"No, I have not." Detective Keating paused, the earlier humbleness having vanished. "Miss Vix and Mr. Smith informed me that you spoke with them."

"I know it was out of turn," Ginny said with a little shrug and smile, but she found that her charm didn't work on Detective Keating the same way that it worked on others.

"Indeed, it was," he said. Then was silent. "But since you helped me here," he said after a moment, "I am willing to overlook it."

"Thank you, detective," Ginny said, and inside she felt relieved. "Neither of them have genuine alibis," she pointed out.

"Yes, I am aware of that."

Ginny sensed that the detective was going to ask her to stay out of the rest of his investigation, and that's just what he did.

"I appreciate your help in this instance, but I will have to ask you to not do that again," Detective Keating said.

Ginny promised him she wouldn't, although she knew that wouldn't stop her.

Keating nodded. "Good day, miss," he said and went on his way.

15

In the evening, the dining car reopened, and Ginny ran into Hendrik near the doorway. She had gone to her room first to tend to Scarlet for a while.

Hendrik grinned at her. "I didn't know if I should try your room or if you would be here. I thought I might find you here," he told her.

"I was wondering the same. What have you been up to? I haven't seen you around."

"I had some business matters to tend to, on the phone and such."

"Oh," Ginny said. "I went by the telephone earlier but didn't see you there."

"I was only on the phone for a while before going into my room."

"Oh, I see."

"What have you been doing?" he asked her.

"I did go see Maureen and that porter about the new murder," Ginny said. "And, of course, Detective Keating found out."

"Was he cross?" Hendrik asked, and she couldn't tell whether he'd asked it in jest.

"I don't think he likes my interfering," she said. "But I can't help but feel he's missing something."

"I know what you mean, it does seem to be taking a long time for him to solve this thing. I'm not surprised the passengers are getting restless."

"Yes, there's that, but I do feel, on the inside that something isn't right with this whole thing. I think something's more obvious than we think."

"What do you mean?" Hendrik asked, seeming interested.

"I'm not sure yet exactly, but it will come to me soon."

"Please, do tell me once it does, I'm curious," Hendrik said.

"I will," Ginny promised.

"Shall we go see if there's a table?" Hendrik asked. The dining car was filling up with passengers who were excited about its reopening.

"Yes, let's," Ginny said.

Hendrik took her arm in his, and they walked inside the lounge. Ginny spotted the mutiny couples as soon as they entered.

"Those passengers, the ones who we overheard discussing a plan to leave the train, are right over there," she told Hendrik.

He started to crane his neck to look, and Ginny said, "No, don't look."

"Already did, sorry," he said. "I don't think they noticed us."

"Oh, I'm sure they did, and they hate us. It's all right, though, I'm sure they've calmed down a bit."

They found a quiet table in the back despite the crowd and had a pleasant meal. Hendrik offered to walk Ginny back to her room afterwards, but she declined.

"I'll be fine," she said.

"Are you sure?" Hendrik asked. "I have to make a telephone call, but it's no trouble at all for me to accompany you first."

"That's all right," she said. "I'm sure I'll be all right."

Truthfully, she felt that having Hendrik so near her room would tempt her to invite him inside, and she didn't feel she was quite ready for that yet.

They parted ways, and Ginny went toward the sleeping car. She stopped and said hello to Mr. Warwick in the corridor.

"How is Mrs. Warwick?" she asked him.

"Still ill, I'm afraid," he replied. "How are you, dear?"

"I'm doing well, thank you."

"I do hope you haven't been following that policeman around more. That's a dreadful business for a young lady to get involved in," he said.

"I'm afraid I find it interesting, Mr. Warwick."

His eyes widened, and he pulled his head back. "You do?"

"Yes, very much."

"We truly are in modern times," Mr. Warwick said. "Goodbye, my dear." He went on his way.

Ginny reached her cabin and unlocked the door. She could hear Scarlet bounding to the floor inside the room. Ginny opened the door and entered the dark room. Scarlet's soft coat circled her legs, and Ginny closed the door and felt for the lamp. She'd left her curtain open, and a tall shadow appeared outside her window and the glint of something long, thin, and sharp.

Ginny gasped. Someone, it looked like the figure of a man, was holding a knife outside her window, trying to frighten her. Ginny slowly walked toward the window, staying out of his view. By the time she reached it and peered to the ground down below, he'd vanished. She looked around to see if there were any newsmen outside, but they had all gone home for the night.

Ginny checked to make sure the window was locked, and seeing it was, she didn't turn on her light because she feared she could be seen outside with it on. She picked up Scarlet in her arms and rushed outside and down the corridor, in search of Detective Keating, but didn't know if he'd left for the evening. She thought about seeking out Hendrik but decided to find the detective first.

Detective Keating stood outside the dining car, speaking to the conductor. He paused when he saw her and saw that she looked distraught.

"Are you all right, miss?" he inquired.

"No, I'm not," Ginny said. "There's a—there was a man outside my cabin window, and he had a knife."

Detective Keating looked noticeably alarmed. "Did you recognize him?"

Ginny shook her head. "I could only see his shadow, but he was tall. I think someone is trying to frighten me because they think I've been snooping around too much."

Detective Keating stared at her.

"Don't you see, this means Maureen and I are innocent because I saw a man," Ginny said.

Detective Keating sighed. Did he think she was making it up?

"Are you on your way home?" she asked him. "I don't mean to trouble you."

"No, miss. I will be spending the night on the train instead of returning home, as part of my investigation. You're quite sure you saw someone?"

"Yes, someone was there."

"Wait here, miss. I will step outside and check the area around your cabin."

Even if he did believe she was telling a lie, he'd decided to humor her anyway. He took off down the corridor.

Ginny nodded and hugged Scarlet close to her as she stood waiting for him to return. She thought about going to Hendrik's room and realized she had never been inside it.

Detective Keating reappeared after a couple of minutes. He looked flustered and annoyed.

"No one is there," he informed her.

"But someone was," Ginny insisted. "I'm telling the truth."

"Yes, yes, of course you think you are."

"Are you suggesting that I might be mad?" Ginny asked.

"I'm not sure, miss. You could very well be, or perhaps you are trying to throw me off your trail by claiming you saw a man and thereby causing me to believe that the culprit isn't you."

"That's absurd," Ginny said with exasperation. "I've done nothing of the sort. I saw a man outside my window, a tall man, and he was holding up a knife for me to see. He was trying to frighten me, I'm sure of it."

"Yes, well, I asked the policeman I have stationed outside the train, and he did not see anything at all, let alone a man with a knife."

"The train is quite long," Ginny asserted. "He might not have seen him. The man must have sneaked past the policeman who missed seeing him. Our culprit is quite cunning, I would imagine, and clever; after all, we haven't caught him yet."

"We?"

"Yes, we, you, whoever." She waited a moment. "You have to believe me." She tried to appeal to his softer side and looked him in the eye. "This man I saw, he could be after me. What if he's on the train?"

"Rest assured you have me to protect you, and I am sure Mr. Bergen as well," Keating said, as though to quell her worry.

"Does that mean you believe me?" Ginny sighed.

"I'm not sure whether I do, but if there is any truth to this matter, you needn't be alarmed because I will keep an eye out. Speaking of which, perhaps the man you saw, if someone really was there, is our porter Smith."

Ginny shook her head. "No, that man Smith is too short to have been the man I saw. The man I saw was quite tall."

"How close were you to the window when you saw this man?"

"I was by my door."

Detective Keating put his finger to his pursed lips and thought. "Perhaps, from the angle you saw him, since you were inside and he was outside, he looked taller," he said after a while.

"No," Ginny said. "I don't believe that's possible. I don't think it was Mr. Smith. It wasn't just the stature that looked tall, the man seemed to have quite a solid build, and Mr. Smith is thin."

Hendrik appeared down the corridor, and Ginny

waved him over. She embraced him, and he rubbed her arm.

"Darling, what's wrong? You have me frightened."

"Oh, Hendrik, it was terrible. There was a man outside my cabin window with a knife."

"How dreadful," Hendrik said and pulled her close. "He must have been trying to scare you into staying away from what's occurred."

"Perhaps I should avoid snooping around from now on."

"It wouldn't be the worst thing," Hendrik agreed. "It's a matter of your safety."

"That's a very fine idea," the detective said.

"Detective Keating thinks it was Smith, the porter, whom I saw, but I'm not as certain," Ginny told Hendrik.

"You did speak to him, questioned him without my permission, and it's likely that angered him," Keating said.

"He was drunk when I saw him," Ginny said. "I don't think he's capable of smoothly planning a murder. He seems much too rash to me."

"Drunk, you say? I will report him to the conductor," Detective Keating said.

"He's probably sobered up by now. I still don't think he was the man I saw."

"I've been looking for you," Hendrik said to Ginny. "I went to your cabin and you weren't there."

"Why were you looking for me?" she asked him.

"I just had a feeling something was wrong."

"How very interesting," Detective Keating remarked. "Perhaps you could use some of your physic abilities, Mr. Bergen, to help me solve this case." He chuckled, and Hendrik shot him daggers with his eyes.

"Regardless," Hendrik said to both of them. "I think our detective here could be right about Smith being the man who you saw outside your window."

Ginny looked at Hendrik. "I'm afraid I don't think it was him," Ginny told him. "I saw a tall man, and Smith isn't tall."

"She saw the man from a distance," Detective Keating told Hendrik. "I've already explained to her how that can distort a person's height."

"The detective could be right," Hendrik said to Ginny.

"I don't agree," Ginny said.

"We could stand here and argue about this all day, but I now have two murders to solve. I've already informed Miss Weltermint that I will keep an eye on things – I won't so much as take a nap – to ensure her safety, and I assume you will do the same." He looked at Hendrik.

"I will, detective," Hendrik said.

"Please see that Miss Weltermint and her cat return to their cabin safely," Detective Keating said to Hendrik, who nodded.

When Detective Keating left, Hendrik turned to her and said, "I'll take you back to your room, Ginny."

He started to loop his arm in hers, but she stopped him.

"Do you want to be part of my investigation on the sly?" she asked him.

"What are you saying?" he asked.

"There's someplace I'd like to go."

He paused, then grinned and said, "You can count me in."

Scripted Murder

Ginny told him about the card with the name *Little Joe's* that she'd found on the first victim, and she gave him the address.

"I'm familiar with this area," Hendrik said, "and I think that address, although it's not a proper address, is in a wooded place fairly close by."

Ginny said, "Let's go there."

"Are you sure that's a good idea? We don't know what this Little Joe's place is."

"It's probably just some restaurant."

"But how are we going to leave when they won't permit us off the train?" Hendrik asked.

"We'll just have to sneak past them." Ginny started off down the corridor, and Hendrik followed. "I need to put Scarlet back in my room first."

"Do you really think we can find a way outside?" he asked her.

"Sure, anything's possible when you set your mind to it. Are you still in?"

He nodded. "I wouldn't miss it."

They reached Ginny's cabin and entered together. Ginny stared at the window but didn't see anyone. Hendrik checked also. She set Scarlet down on the bed and went over to the window and closed the curtain.

Ginny went to her suitcase and took out a red evening dress. "I want to change in case the place is fancy," she said. "We wouldn't want to look out of place."

"I don't have a tuxedo," Hendrik said.

"That's all right, you look quite sharp in your suit."

Ginny changed behind the little closet door and freshened up her makeup and fixed her hair. She chose sensible shoes because she figured she might have to walk far, and they were on their way.

Ginny said goodbye to Scarlet and locked the door on her way out. They tried the exit closest to the sleeping car, where there wasn't a guard, but found the door bolted so tightly they'd never get it open. It was late at night, and most of the other passengers had retired to their rooms for the evening. They casually walked down the corridor toward the quiet smoking car, with one lone passenger inside, reading a newspaper, and past the exit there, where a guard stood watch. The man looked unlikely to drift off to sleep any time soon despite the late hour.

The other exits they tried, near the dining car and the lounge, both had attentive guards. The last remaining exit was located near the conductor's booth, and Ginny reasoned it would also be guarded. She thought about climbing out through a window, but Hendrik would be much too large to fit through one. They reached the exit by the booth, and a guard sat on a chair in front of it, with his chin dropped down to his chest, asleep.

Ginny gestured to the man. "He's sleeping," she whispered to Hendrik. "Let's sneak past him."

Hendrik nodded, and went first. He reached the exit door, and Ginny winced as he attempted to turn the handle and it seemed locked. The handle made a squeaking sound, and the sleeping guard stirred.

Ginny motioned to the guard and gestured for Hendrik to be careful. She searched the guard's uniform with her gaze and pointed to the key on the guard's belt loop.

Hendrik reached around the chair and attempted to unhook the key from the man's belt. The man moved slightly. Ginny put her hand to her mouth and held her breath. At any moment, someone, another guard, Detective Keating, could walk by the quiet area they were in, so they didn't have a lot of time to carry out the task.

Hendrik slowly got the key off the man's belt loop. He put it in the lock, and gently turned the handle and the door opened. He pocketed the key and motioned for Ginny to follow. She tip-toed past the guard, and Hendrik held her hand.

Together they climbed over the railing, jumped off, and landed in the grass. The cool, fresh air hit Ginny's face. They stood up and dusted themselves off, and she breathed in the smell of the air with delight. It had been much too long since she smelled fresh air. Had they run into Detective Keating inside the train, he would have suspected they were up to something and questioned why she was dressed so nicely. Ginny exhaled.

"I am glad we didn't see Detective—" Ginny started to say, and Hendrik gestured for her to be silent.

They hid in the shadows while a policeman patrolled the open area outside the train. Once he had gone farther down the train, Hendrik gestured for her to step into the woods at their left.

"Come on," he said.

They walked through the dense forest, with Ginny grateful she'd worn the proper shoes, and heard the cries of animals in the nighttime. Hendrik held her close as they walked, and soon they reached a quiet road, the darkness lit by the stars and silver moonlight.

"How will we remember which rail car we exited?" Ginny asked him.

"It was by a large oak tree; that will be our marker."

"How far away do you think it is?" Ginny asked.

"Not too far, but far enough that we ought to hitch-hike the rest of the way."

Ginny didn't like the idea, but they seemed to have few options. "I hope someone will come by." She looked around. "I don't see or hear any vehicles."

"They'll come eventually, I'm sure," Hendrik said. "Hopefully, Keating won't solve the case while we're away and the train will take off without us."

16

Ginny saw the glare of lights, and a truck came slowly down the road. Hendrik waved at the driver, and the vehicle stopped.

The man opened his window. "Are you folks all right?" he asked them. He appeared to be some kind of a farmer.

"Actually, we could use a ride," Hendrik replied.

The man seemed to be thinking for a moment. "Sure, get in."

There were no seats in the back, so they had to sit in front with the driver. Hendrik sat next to the man, and Ginny sat on the other side of Hendrik.

Hendrik gave him the name of the place and the address, and for a while, the man didn't say much as he drove. Inside, the truck smelled of tobacco.

Then he said, "I own a farm outside of the village. Did your vehicle break down a ways back?" he asked them.

"We came from the train, actually," Ginny said. "The one that's stopped."

"I read about that in the papers. I thought you

folks were supposed to stay on it until the murder is solved."

"We broke free," Hendrik replied with a grin.

"You wanted to get out and enjoy yourselves for a while?" The man smiled as if he understood.

"Yes, something like that," Ginny said.

"Little Joe's is the kind of place where folks can enjoy themselves. 'Course I don't partake in that kind of enjoyment myself. It's a bit rough of a place for a refined lady such as yourself, if you don't mind my saying, ma'am," he told Ginny.

"Thank you, but I imagine I'll be all right. Besides," she said, touching Hendrik's arm, "I have good company."

The man made a sharp right into some woods and continued on a narrow dirt road. He shut off his lights. Ginny said with alarm, "Are you sure this is the way?"

"Yes, ma'am. It's in the woods. I'll have to drop you off in a moment because that's what you're supposed to do when going there. They don't like cars being parked nearby because it draws too much attention." He slowed down his truck and stopped at the side of the road.

Ginny and Hendrik thanked him for the ride and exited. The man gestured to up the road from inside the car.

"It's up that a-ways," he spoke through the open window.

They nodded and continued on foot up the road. They reached a ramshackle wood building with a hand-painted sign: *Little Joe's*.

"This doesn't look like much," Hendrik remarked.

Ginny shrugged. "Let's go inside and see. I wonder why a seeming sophisticated man like Mr. O'Connor had the card for an establishment like this in his pocket."

"I think it's a gin joint, a speakeasy," Hendrik said. "In the middle of nowhere. People from the city probably drive out here to drink. That's why it doesn't have a proper address."

"You haven't ever been here, have you?" Ginny remarked with a slight smile.

"Heavens no. I like a drink once in a while, but this place seems even too wild for me."

They walked closer, and Ginny could hear jazz music coming from inside the place. Hendrik motioned that he would enter first, just in case.

He opened the door, walked halfway inside, took a look around, and gestured for her to enter. Inside the place, the loud, lively music filled Ginny's ears. They paid a fee to a heavily made-up older woman in a sparkly blue dress, sitting on a stool at the front of the room.

"If you have any guns, please leave them here," the woman said, her voice sounding coarse as she indicated a bucket on the floor by her feet, which contained a few pistols.

Ginny stared in surprise, and she and Hendrik shook their heads.

Further inside, the place was more sophisticated, with a delicate chandelier and an elegant bar with a glistening mirror behind it. There were numerous well-dressed men and women about who seemed like city folks, dancing to the fast jazz music or drinking and laughing and chatting at the small tables of the cigarette smoke-filled room. Ginny had visited many such places in California over the years, and Hendrik also seemed experienced with them, and so they blended right into the crowd.

A few men in the corner wore dark suits and menacing expressions. Ginny thought they looked like bootleggers or gangsters and seemed to be affiliated with the place, possibly one was the owner. They stared at Hendrik and seemed alarmed by his presence, which wasn't too surprising since he was a large, intimidating looking man.

"Let's dance," Hendrik said and pulled her onto the floor, where he twirled her then held her close when the music slowed, and the voice of the sultry singer on the stage softened.

Ginny looked around as they danced, and many of the people at the speakeasy seemed to know one another. Hendrik pulled her in tightly when the song neared its end and placed his lips to hers for a kiss. Ginny's heart raced, and she accepted the kiss. Romance was happening again for her, and so soon after Paul.

Hendrik smiled handsomely at her when the song stopped and the singer took a break. The band played an instrumental jazz beat in the background.

"Let's get a drink, shall we?" Hendrik said.

Ginny nodded. "I'd like that."

He took her hand in his and led her over to the bar toward the back of the establishment. As they waited for their booze drinks, they attempted to strike up a conversation with some of the other patrons at the bar.

"Have you been coming here long?" Ginny asked a man in a tuxedo.

The man shrugged.

"Do you know who owns the place?" she asked.

The man murmured, "I don't know," and ignored her and started talking to the woman alongside Ginny.

Hendrik asked another man and the woman with him the same question, and they both just shook their heads. Ginny searched for an employee to speak with but only saw the intimidating men in the suits, and they seemed unlikely to be cooperative. But there was the bartender, a large, jovial-appearing man.

"Let's ask him," Ginny said to Hendrik. "He might know something. He probably sees all the goings-on here."

"Yes, that's a good idea," he replied. "I'll ask him when he serves us. Perhaps a little incentive will help."

They waited a few more moments for their drinks, and Ginny listened as Hendrik tapped his fingers on the bar to the sound of the music.

"Here you go, for the lady and the gent," the bartender said and set their drinks down in front of them on the bar.

Ginny and Hendrik thanked the man and they sipped their drinks. The booze made her feel lightheaded and closer to Hendrik.

"Who owns this place anyway?" Hendrik asked the bartender after a while.

The bartender shrugged.

Hendrik took some bills out of his pocket and set them on the shiny wood bar. He looked at the bills and then at the bartender. "I would appreciate some information," he said.

The man seemed less friendly. "What do you want to know that for?" He watched Hendrik and Ginny.

Hendrik put his hand over the money and started to pull it back towards him, as though he would take it back.

The bartender stopped him, picked up the money, and nodded as he pocketed it.

"Up until recently, it was owned by a man named O'Connor. 'Little Joe' is his nickname."

Ginny could feel a lump in her throat. "William O'Connor?" she asked.

The bartender nodded. "His middle name was Joseph, nickname Joe. He was a short fellow. He was also a decent boss."

"He was murdered," Hendrik said.

"On the train, the one that's stopped. Have you heard what happened?" Ginny asked the bartender.

"I heard about that, yeah, but didn't know it was Little Joe who got it."

"Is there anything more you can tell us?" Ginny asked.

"That's all I can tell you. The new owners won't like me talking about this." The bartender eyed the gangster types, who Ginny saw were watching them speak with the bartender. He walked to the end of the bar.

"Prohibition," Ginny said to Hendrik. "Perhaps Mr. O'Connor sold this place because he knew it would possibly be ending soon."

"Do you mean that maybe he had a tip from someone in the government confirming the speculation was true?" Hendrik asked.

"Possibly," Ginny said. "Perhaps that has something to do with his death. Of course, that wouldn't explain the second murder."

The men in the dark suits in the corner gestured for the bartender to come speak with them, and he stepped out from behind the bar. The group watched

Ginny and Hendrik, who were drinking, as they spoke to him.

"Something's going on," Ginny said.

"I noticed, and I don't like the looks of it. Perhaps we should get out of here soon."

The bartender returned to his place, and the men in suits conferred with some other men, who were dressed like them and had similar tough expressions, and then they all retreated into the back through a side door.

"Is everything all right?" Hendrik asked the bartender.

He looked at them and didn't say anything, but his expression seemed bleak.

"Come on," Hendrik suddenly said to Ginny. "Let's get out of here." He grabbed her hand, and she set her drink down on the bar.

The men in suits appeared from the back in a greater number than before and started to approach them. Some of them stepped to the front of the cluster, each with one of their hands behind their backs, concealing something out of Ginny's view. One of the men gestured to the woman on the stool at the front to stop Ginny and Hendrik.

"I think they have guns behind their backs," Hendrik said.

Ginny gasped. They dashed past the woman just as she rose and made it out the front door. The door shut. Ginny heard it open again as the men exited and ran after them.

Hendrik steered her toward the woods surrounding the place, and they bolted around the dense, tall trees. The men followed them. They made many turns in the forest, and after a while, Ginny no longer heard the crunch of footsteps.

"I think we've lost them," Hendrik declared.

They slowed down, and Ginny panted. "Thank God. That was utterly dreadful. You don't know how scared I was, darling."

Ginny realized she'd started to use the term of endearment with him also.

Hendrik put his arm around her and hugged her close and kissed her hair. "I am glad you're all right," he whispered.

The forest acted as a shortcut of sorts, and soon they reached the road where they'd hitchhiked earlier.

"I doubt we'll see that farmer again," Ginny said. "So we'll have to walk back to the train. Thankfully, I wore comfortable shoes."

"I could always carry you," Hendrik offered, and Ginny laughed.

"I do wonder why we were chased," she said.

"Perhaps they thought I was a detective," Hendrik said. "In this suit, I do look like one."

"Or perhaps they didn't like us asking the bartender about Mr. O'Connor," Ginny said.

They went a different way back and reached the quiet village in the area near the train that was lined with dark houses, some of which had a small light shining from the inside. A policeman still patrolled by the train in the distance.

"We'll have to sneak past him again," Ginny told Hendrik.

"We'll wait until he's farther down the train and make a run for it."

Ginny nodded.

Once the man went out of view, she and Hendrik

sprinted to the train and approached the car by the large oak tree. Hendrik climbed up and over the railing and tried to open the door, but it wouldn't budge. He removed the key from his pocket and quietly inserted it in the lock and turned it. He pushed open the door and helped Ginny climb up into the car.

"Ahem," Detective Keating cleared his throat inside the train. He'd been standing by the door, waiting for them.

Ginny stared at Keating quietly, unsure of what to say, and Hendrik followed her inside. He dusted off his trousers.

"Detective," he said. "What a surprise to see you here."

"Mr. Bergen. Miss Weltermint. I don't believe I have to convey how disappointed I am in both of you. You decided to sneak off, when here I thought you were interested in helping me maintain order." He scolded them for stealing the crewman's key. "The man woke up and noticed it missing from his belt, and being the good man he is, he reported it to me."

"Detective Keating," Ginny said to him. "I found a card on the first victim for a place named Little Joe's. Hendrik and I were just there."

"You went through the man's pockets?" the detective spoke with irritation.

"I'm surprised you didn't investigate the card yourself. You didn't, did you?"

"I am aware of it, yes, but I do not believe it's significant."

"Will you be investigating it now? Something very odd is going on here," she said. "We were chased out of the place – it's a speakeasy – by men with guns."

"You're admitting to visiting a forbidden establishment?" Detective Keating said. "Did you imbibe?"

"Of course we didn't," Hendrik lied.

The detective seemed to be sniffing them for the scent of booze.

"They probably chased you out because you're outsiders," he said. "Those types of places are filled with danger."

"We found out that Mr. O'Connor once owned the gin joint, and so it's possible he was a gangster," Ginny said.

"That won't be needed, Miss Weltermint," Detective Keating replied.

"Why is that, detective?" Ginny asked sweetly.

"Because it doesn't matter at this point. In your absence, we discovered that one of the people aboard the train has a criminal conviction for robbery. Obviously, this interests us since some money appears to have been taken from Mr. O'Connor's room. A professional would know not to leave fingerprints behind in both instances. We now have our prime suspect."

"How are they connected to the second victim?" Ginny asked.

"We are establishing that," the detective replied. "Once we've wrapped everything up, the train will resume its journey, which should be shortly."

"This prime suspect," Hendrik said, "is it the porter or Maureen Vix?"

"No, his name is John Reed, and he is a third-class passenger, a veteran of the war." Detective Keating looked at Ginny. "Surely, you'll be pleased that you are no longer under suspicion, Miss Weltermint, and neither are the others."

Scripted Murder

"That's great to hear," Hendrik told the detective. He looked at Ginny. "Isn't it, Ginny?"

"It is, indeed." Ginny managed a half-smile. Yet something did not feel right to her.

"Are we in trouble for sneaking out, detective?" Hendrik asked.

"I'm in a good mood tonight, so I'll overlook it," Detective Keating stated. "As long as both of you promise not to cause me any more trouble for the remainder of the time I am aboard."

Hendrik and Ginny both agreed.

Detective Keating held out his hand, and Hendrik gave him the key. "The crewman will be relieved. He felt quite badly that he'd slipped up."

Ginny and Hendrik parted ways with the detective. Hendrik kissed her again.

"Say, that was quite exciting, wasn't it? With you by my side," he said.

"Indeed, it was," Ginny replied.

She let go of his hand and retreated into her room and checked on Scarlet, who was sleeping.

"Hello, sweet girl," she said.

17

The late night had turned into early morning. Ginny thought about resting for a while but changed her clothes instead and went to go see Maureen in second class.

Ginny knocked on the girl's cabin, and Maureen opened the door.

"I apologize for it being so early," Ginny said.

"It's all right, I've been up reading. The other girls are still asleep." She spoke to Ginny while holding the door open and had a book in her other hand.

"I wanted to tell you myself as soon as I heard—we're no longer under suspicion, according to Detective Keating."

Maureen dropped her book to the ground in shock, and one of the girls stirred in the room. Maureen left the book on the floor and embraced Ginny.

"Oh, ma'am, I'm so relieved," she said.

Ginny patted her back. "I am as well."

Maureen looked at her. "I'm so sorry for being angry with you before. It was out of character for me. I don't know what came over me. If my mother saw me like that, she'd be very ashamed." She put her chin to her chest and looked at the floor.

"It's all right, Maureen. All is forgiven," Ginny said with a smile. "I'm sorry as well."

"Ma'am—Ginny—who did they arrest?" Maureen asked her after a moment as she picked up her book from the floor.

"They have a suspect, but as far as I know, no formal arrest has been made."

"Are we in danger?" Maureen asked with fear thick in her voice.

"I wouldn't think so," Ginny said and patted the girl's hand.

"I am so glad it's over," Maureen said.

"So am I," Ginny said, but deep down inside something didn't feel right to her about Detective Keating's suspect. "You have an audition to prepare for after all."

"You're still arranging that for me, after how rude I was to you?" Maureen asked with surprise.

"Why, of course, Maureen. I always do what I promise."

"Oh, ma'am—Ginny—how kind you are to me. Thank you." Maureen's eyes sparkled with admiration.

Ginny left Maureen to return to her room and rest for a while and tend to Scarlet. After a few hours of sleep, she bathed and dressed and got Scarlet ready to go out. She left her room and went toward the lounge to get a cup of coffee, thinking that she might see Hendrik there. Detective Keating walked ahead of her in the corridor, carrying a cup of tea.

"Hello, detective," she said.

"Miss Weltermint, it's nice to see you again so soon after your escape. Good morning."

She grinned at his attempt at a joke. "Where are you off to?" she asked him.

"I'm on my way to third class to resume my questioning of Mr. Reed. I stopped to get a refreshment." He held up the tea. "One of my policemen is with Mr. Reed at the moment. I anticipate that any hour now the train will be able to resume."

"That should come as a relief to the passengers. I don't believe I've ever heard of this John Reed fellow," Ginny said pryingly.

"I doubt you would have since he is in third class and you are in first, miss. He's an older fellow, a war veteran, as I mentioned. He's on his way to a job in California, while his wife remains in New York."

"He sounds like a decent fellow. How did you come to suspect him? Surely, now that it's all over, you can at least tell me how it happened. You've piqued my curiosity."

The detective nodded. "Now that it is all over, I shall indulge your curiosity. I shall tell you because I guess it does somewhat concern you." He cleared his throat. "His name came up because Mr. Smith, the porter, who I'd been keeping an eye on, knew Mr. Reed back in New York and told me about his past, and when I looked into it, I found a theft conviction for the man in New York and that he had been to jail for it. As you know, the first victim was robbed."

Ginny wondered about the porter's real motive for telling Detective Keating about John Reed.

"Mr. Smith, who knows Mr. Reed, has informed me that Mr. Reed asked him to leave the note in your room and turn on the record player for money, to frighten you into ceasing your snooping."

"Why didn't Mr. Smith tell us this earlier?" Ginny asked.

"He claimed he was only revealing it now because he knows the man and he was paid. We've made Mr. Reed provide us with a handwriting sample, and it is quite similar to the note left for you, miss."

"Could it be coincidental?" Ginny asked.

"No, I don't think so."

"Then what was his motive for killing Mr. Doyle?"

"There is a connection. Mr. Reed insists that he sneaked into first class to try to steal something, and he walked by Mr. O'Connor's cabin and saw the door open and the body and thought about looking for something to steal, but he claims that he walked inside, changed his mind, and left. But he admits to bumping into Mr. Doyle on his way out of first class, and the man looked at him strangely because he didn't look like he belonged there. That must have been what Mr. Doyle wanted to discuss with me. I believe he is lying about Mr. O'Connor and that he actually robbed and killed the man and then killed Mr. Doyle for seeing him in the vicinity. So, Mr. Reed had motive to kill both men. I believe he will confess and sign a statement very soon."

"I see," Ginny said. "Yes, I guess that makes sense."

"Pardon me, miss?"

"Doesn't it seem a little too neat to you? I can't help but feel that something is missing."

"I understand that you fancy yourself some kind of amateur sleuth, miss, but I am a genuine detective."

"I don't doubt your abilities," she said when she saw that she had inadvertently insulted him. "Thank you for telling me, detective," she said to end the conversation.

Keating nodded and continued on his way down to third class.

"Something *isn't* right," Ginny said to herself.

She returned to her room and put Scarlet inside. Next, she headed to third class. She didn't see Detective Keating in the third-class car and reasoned he had retreated somewhere to resume his questioning of Reed, but she needed to find out where. Before she could, a man dressed in a plain shirt and trousers with a cap on his head, ran into her in the corridor. He seemed to be fleeing from someone. He looked at her.

"What are you doing here? Are you in first class?" he asked, staring at her fine clothes.

She nodded.

"You should be good enough to make them listen to me," he said.

"Pardon me?" she asked.

He took out a knife and pointed it at her. "Come with me," he said.

Ginny gulped and recoiled but had no choice but to listen to him as he ordered her down the corridor, checked the kitchen car, and ordered her inside.

Ginny stepped into the quiet car with him directly behind her, pointing his knife.

"What's your name, sir?" she asked him.

"John Reed," he replied.

"I know who you are, Mr. Reed."

"How come?"

"Detective Keating told me. I was the person who found the first body."

"I didn't kill him or the other one," Reed insisted. "That's where I escaped from; Detective Keating was trying to get me to sign a confession. I won't let you go until the police leave me alone!"

"I believe you, Mr. Reed," Ginny shouted calmly. "I think that your being the culprit is a little too easy. In fact, that's the reason I'm here in the first place. I was on my way to see if I could find you to talk."

"They think they can pin it on me just because I served time for robbery," he said loudly. "I only did that robbery all those years ago because I was desperate. It was after I got back from the war. I was homeless at the time and starving, and so I took a man's wallet at a café. I'm innocent in these murders."

"What about the note left for me, did you have anything to do with that?" Ginny asked.

"I never left a note for you. I don't even know you."

Ginny was facing Reed, who had his back to the door and so he didn't see it when Hendrik approached.

"Leave her alone!" Hendrik yelled from the doorway.

He grappled with Reed from behind. The knife clanged on the floor as Hendrik disarmed him.

"Are you all right?" he asked Ginny.

She nodded, but she was a bit disappointed he'd entered the picture because she was sure she'd been about to get closer to the truth.

Detective Keating entered the kitchen car from the corridor. "I've been looking for you," he told Reed. "What's going on here?"

"He was holding Ginny hostage," Hendrik told him. "He had a knife." Hendrik kicked the knife on the floor with his foot.

"I'm not surprised," Detective Keating said. "This is John Reed, my prime suspect."

"That explains a lot," Hendrik said.

"I'm innocent," Reed insisted to the two men.

"I think that what you just did to Miss Weltermint, plus your old conviction, proves otherwise," Detective Keating stated.

"I wouldn't be so sure," Ginny interrupted. "Mr. Reed explained to me that he only took that man's wallet years ago because he was homeless after his service and was hungry."

"Excuse me, miss, but this is a detective's work." Keating handcuffed Reed, who turned to look at Ginny.

"I'm very sorry, ma'am, for frightening you. I panicked," he said.

Ginny turned to Hendrik. "What about you, don't you think there's something off about this whole thing?"

"Darling, he put a knife to you."

"Would you risk sending an innocent man to prison for the rest of his life or the gallows?"

Hendrik squeezed her shoulder. "I don't think him being innocent is possible, Ginny."

Detective Keating picked up the knife. "He must have also sneaked outside to your window at night to frighten you with this."

"It's my knife, but I never scared her with it before now," Reed said.

"Yes, how convenient," Detective Keating remarked.

"Who gave my name to you anyhow?" Reed asked the detective.

"It was a porter."

"I'm being framed," Reed insisted.

"That's unlikely," the detective replied. "Now, if you'll excuse me, I shall take this man away," he said to Ginny and Hendrik. "I am sorry for the fright, miss."

"What are you doing in this part of the train anyway?" Ginny asked Hendrik as the detective left with Reed.

"I was looking for you. I heard you shouting."

Ginny exited the kitchen with Hendrik and trailed behind Detective Keating leading John Reed away. Two policemen joined the detective in escorting Reed, and many of the other passengers took notice of the occurrence and lined up to watch.

Ginny and Hendrik watched from the corridor as an exhausted John Reed signed the confession in the smoking room under Detective Keating's eye. Ginny looked at Hendrik, who seemed calm as he watched, but inside, her heart was racing with the thought that something didn't feel right with the situation. The two policemen with Keating took John Reed away and off the train, and Ginny could see that outside the newspapermen were photographing them during the escort.

Passengers murmured and discussed the incident among themselves, and Detective Keating motioned for them to settle.

"Ladies and gentlemen, I am pleased to say that we have solved the crimes, and so your journey will continue," he told everyone who had gathered to watch.

The passengers breathed a collective sigh of relief, and some cheered and whistled. Hendrik looked at her and grinned, but Ginny didn't much feel like celebrating. She couldn't help but think that Mr. Reed could be innocent.

The passengers returned to their business, and Detective Keating approached Ginny and Hendrik.

"Goodbye, Mr. Bergen and Miss Weltermint," he said.

"You're leaving already?" Ginny asked.

"Yes, my work here is done."

"Why not stay for a drink?" Hendrik said.

"I'm afraid the missus is eager for me to return home, so I must decline, but thank you."

Ginny and Hendrik watched him exit the train.

"I doubt we'll ever see him again," Hendrik said.

"You're probably right. I must say, I didn't like him very much at first, but he turned out to be okay," Ginny said.

She looked out the window as the newsmen who had gathered began to depart one by one, and she felt the train starting and the motion of the wheels as they continued onwards.

"Shall we get a drink in the lounge?" Hendrik asked her.

"Yes, I'd like that," Ginny said.

They returned to her room to get Scarlet first and went to the lounge and retreated inside for a few hours.

Nighttime arrived, and the cook had prepared a celebratory dinner for all of the passengers in their respective dining cars. Ginny and Hendrik returned Scarlet to Ginny's room and enjoyed a relaxing meal together.

"I have a confession to make," he told her during dessert.

Ginny put down her fork on her cake plate and looked at him.

"I don't really work for Blue Autos," Hendrik said.

"Oh?" Ginny said, startled.

"I work for the Dutch government. I'm on my way

to California for a meeting with some delegates. The meeting is secret, which is why I had to lie to you about my occupation. But I've developed feelings for you, and I can't bear not being honest with you."

That explained his remark to Detective Keating about him being a good judge of character.

"Are you joking?" she asked him just to be certain.

He shook his head.

"All right," she said, getting slightly more comfortable with the idea, and intrigued. "How fascinating. Do tell more."

Hendrik reached for and held her hand across the table. "Perhaps later I can, when we spend time together in California."

"I look forward to it. You know," Ginny said while still holding his hand. "Now that I know this about you and your experience, I think I ought to tell you my feelings about Mr. Reed's arrest. I'd like your opinion on the matter."

He nodded at her to continue.

"I'm not comfortable with the whole thing," Ginny said. "I just feel that man could be innocent."

"Darling," Hendrik said soothingly. "The man has a criminal record and took you hostage. You want to believe the best about people, and I admire you for that, but I do believe Detective Keating's caught the culprit."

Ginny nodded and sighed. "I'm sure you're right, of course." But her stomach still fluttered with anxiety over the matter.

"Now, what shall we do with the rest of our evening?" Hendrik asked. "I heard that some people are gathering in the smoking room to play cards after dinner."

"That might be interesting." Ginny paused. "You know," she thought aloud. "I've never seen your room. You've seen mine plenty of times."

"Would you like to see it?" he asked her.

The idea sounded quite brazen, yet, seeking to ease some of her anxiety, she nodded, and because she was curious. "Yes, I'd like that," she replied.

After dessert, they exited the dining car and went down the corridor to the sleeping car, where they approached Hendrik's cabin.

He opened the door with his key.

"You lock your door," she remarked.

"Yes, when I'm not inside. After everything that's happened, I thought it would be a good idea. One of the policemen was suggesting it to the passengers the other day."

"Oh, I see."

He motioned for her to enter the room first, and inside his cabin, it looked identical to hers.

"It looks just like mine," she said.

Hendrik closed the door. He pulled her close to him, tilted his head, and kissed her tenderly.

"Spend the night with me," he whispered into her ear.

She looked at him, gave him a smile, and nodded.

18

Ginny awoke to the sound of someone moving about the room. She felt for Hendrik beside her in bed but found his place empty. She glanced toward the curtain and could see daylight just approaching and entering the room in vibrant streaks.

Hendrik paced around the room and seemed to be looking for a place to put—or hide—something. Ginny quietly sat up in bed. Through the sparse light, it looked as though Hendrik held a gun. He must have had it because of his government work. Had he had it on him the whole time?

She looked to her right and saw a note at the bedside, a reminder about something. Ginny suppressed a gasp as she squinted and read it. The handwriting looked familiar and nearly identical to the person who had left her the note. She had been too distracted last night to notice it. Ginny struggled to maintain composure and be still as Hendrik walked about the room with the object that looked like a gun.

No wonder Scarlet hadn't liked him; she had sensed something was off about him. John Reed's handwriting similarity had to have been a coincidence, and Hendrik must have paid the porter Smith to leave the note. But why had the porter implicated John Reed?

Yet, she had developed feelings for Hendrik, especially after they had spent the night together, and what if she was wrong? There was just one way to find out.

"Was it you the whole time?" she asked, getting up from the bed. She couldn't see his face clearly in the shadows.

Hendrik turned to face her with his gun in hand. "I knew you'd probably figure it out eventually. But I was hoping you wouldn't."

"You lied to me," she said.

"My real name is Hendrik Visser, but most people I work for call me the 'Dutch Butcher.'"

Ginny stepped back from him. "Why did you kill Mr. O'Connor?"

"The Irish mob paid me to. Mr. O'Connor was a former high-ranking mob member who had testified against their boss in exchange for his freedom. He had been trying to flee to California to escape the New York mob's wrath."

"And the meeting with the delegates you told me about, was that all a lie?"

Hendrik shook his head. "I took care of Mr. O'Connor on my way to meet them because it was very convenient for me. I work for various people, including governments."

"And the robbery?" Ginny asked as she tried to remain composed.

"I took money from O'Connor's room so that it would look like one."

"Why were we chased at the speakeasy?"

"I think the mob boss must want me dead to cover his tracks. If I had known he was going to be there, then I never would have gone there with you."

"What about the business card I saw you give Detective Keating?"

"It was one of the fake ones I carry."

"You don't really live in New York, do you?" Ginny said, unable to conceal the fear in her voice.

Hendrik shook his head.

"You paid the porter and threatened him so that he'd leave me the note you wrote," Ginny said, and Hendrik nodded. "Why did you kill Mr. Doyle?" she asked.

"I had no choice. I strangled him because the man had questioned whether I really worked for Blue Automobiles when we had a conversation. You see, his company did business with the engineering department of Blue Autos, and he had never heard of me. I felt that he might tell the police this after Mr. O'Connor's body was found and I'd come under suspicion, so I had to kill him."

That must have been what Mr. Doyle had wanted to speak with Detective Keating about.

Ginny moved farther away from him and closer to the door. "I can't believe you went along with blaming that poor man for your crimes."

"I had to do it to protect myself," Hendrik said. "But everything I told you about my childhood and about my engagement was true. I care about you, Ginny. I was very concerned when Keating suspected you because I didn't want anything to happen to you. You see, I really like you, Ginny, that part wasn't a lie. It's very unfortunate I have to do this." He pointed the gun at her.

"Someone will hear you if you shoot me," she told him. The fact that she had once trusted him gave her the chills now.

Hendrik shook his head. "Not with all the train noise." He paused. "Look at it this way: After your death, your true identity can finally be revealed."

Ginny had slowly backed up to the door. She quickly turned and unlocked it and bolted down the corridor, barefoot and in her undergarments. It was very early in the morning, and no other passengers were up. The crew was either distracted running the train or asleep at that hour.

She could hear Hendrik coming after her down the corridor and glanced over her shoulder to see him running at her with his gun. She spotted an exit and went toward it and found it opened. She dashed outside and could feel the warm air the moving train created blowing past her and making her hair fly. Ginny stood alongside the railing and looked down at the grass and dirt ground passing by fast below. It all seemed blurry. She heard Hendrik opening the door and coming after her. The sun hadn't fully risen, but in the distance, she saw what looked like a lake, shining in the faint light. She remembered that Hendrik couldn't swim. Ginny grappled with the railing and climbed over it. She closed her eyes and jumped.

She landed on the grass, but pain shot through her legs. She looked up in a haze of discomfort and saw Hendrik making his way over the railing and jumping off the train to follow her with his gun in his hand. Ginny sprang up and ran toward the lake bordered by a verdant forest. She ran so fast through the woods, darting between the trees, that it felt as though someone was pushing on her chest. Ginny reached the rocky shore and winced as she walked across in her bare feet. She looked behind her and spotted Hendrik approaching.

Ginny dove into the water, cold but not freezing, and kept swimming away from the shore, where Hendrik stood, trying to shoot her in the water. She hadn't gone swimming in a long time, and her arms throbbed with each careful stroke she made in the water, ducking out of the way of his bullets, and then she submerged herself and swam completely underwater.

Even under the water, she heard a great sound, what sounded like the train stopping quickly. She put her head out of the water and, still swimming away, turned to see a figure, a man, running toward the lake. As he got closer, she saw that it was Detective Keating. Ginny stopped swimming and dodged a bullet as she flailed her arms to warn him about Hendrik, but she imagined he could hear the gunshots.

Detective Keating approached the shore, and Ginny could hear him shouting at Hendrik. She watched and winced from the water as the two men grappled with each other. After a few moments, the detective managed to disarm him. He placed Hendrik in handcuffs and handed him over to another policeman who had arrived.

Ginny swam back to the shore, and Detective Keating helped her out of the water. Some more policemen arrived and escorted Hendrik away. He looked back at her and grinned and shrugged, and she glared at him.

Detective Keating looked away from Ginny's state of undress as they walked back to the stopped train.

The night had fully left, and the sun illuminated the green around them. They reached the train, and a few passengers had exited the stopped train, some in dressing gowns, to see what had happened. They stared at the soaked Ginny in shock and whispered to one another. Ginny followed Detective Keating onboard.

"Fetch her a towel," he said to one of his policemen.

Ginny knew that the story would be in the newspapers the next day, and there would also be a write up in the gossip columns: *Paul Blair's Former Flame Escapes Killer Romance*. She would have to telephone her mother about it before that happened.

The policeman returned with the towel, and Ginny wrapped it around herself. Her hair dripped on her shoulders.

"I had my doubts. But how did you know?" she asked Detective Keating.

"I stayed behind with some of my policemen just in case because I, too, had some doubts. I never really left. I handed Mr. Reed over to my other policemen and got on board again. I will admit that I still suspected you or one of the others somewhat, or possibly someone else. Of course, I was wrong, and I was also wrong about lady detectives. I do sincerely apologize, Miss Weltermint."

"I accept your apology, detective. There's something you should know about me. I'm actually a screenwriter."

He raised his eyebrows. "Professionally?"

Ginny nodded, and she assumed he would scowl, but he gave her a real smile. So he wasn't so surly after all.

"I assume you'll write about what has happened," he said.

"At first, I thought I would, but now I'm not quite as sure."

A policeman came up to the detective and spoke into his ear then left.

"I have been informed that we found a knife in Mr. Bergen's room, and a piece of wire."

Ginny sighed in disappointment at the way things with Hendrik had turned out. After a few moments, Detective Keating parted ways with her.

"How will you get home? We aren't in your village any longer," Ginny spoke with concern.

"I shall be just fine. Goodbye, Miss Weltermint. We are unlikely to see each other again."

Ginny gave him a small smile. "I wouldn't be so sure. I've always wanted to come back to New York and move to the countryside to take a break from Hollywood for a bit. I think the time has come. Of course, I'll have to go home to California as planned to make arrangements."

She had friends in Hollywood who could keep an eye on Maureen.

Detective Keating actually smiled. "I've changed my mind about retirement."

"What will happen to Mr. Reed?" Ginny asked.

"He will be released and his confession thrown out. The similar handwriting was merely coincidental."

A man dashed past them toward the exit, and the policemen grabbed him before he could leave. Detective Keating gestured for the policemen to bring the man, who Ginny now saw was Smith, over to him. The detective turned from Ginny to speak with the porter, and one of the policemen put handcuffs on him and escorted him off the train.

"Mr. Smith has admitted that Mr. Bergen paid him to leave the note in your room and turn on the record player. Apparently, Mr. Smith is in love with John Reed's wife, who is still in New York, and had been trying to get him out of the picture, so after some deliberation, he came up with a plan and decided to provide his name."

"What will happen to Hendrik?" Ginny asked. "The mob is after him."

"That shouldn't concern you, miss, but I can assure you that we will make certain he is safe in prison."

Ginny once more said goodbye to Detective Keating and returned to her room to bathe and change. She'd left her clothes in Hendrik's room, which would probably be filled with policemen at the moment, so she would get them later.

A few hours later, the policemen cleared out of the train, which started again and continued on. Ginny and Scarlet made their way to the smoking room and took a seat near the Warwicks. She inquired about Mrs. Warwick's health and heard that the woman was feeling better. Ginny spotted Maureen in the distance and waved, and the girl gave her a sympathetic smile.

She'd had quite an adventure.

Book 2 in *The Screenwriter and the Detective* series coming soon.

Dear reader,

We hope you enjoyed reading *Scripted Murder*. Please take a moment to leave a review, even if it's a short one. Your opinion is important to us.

Discover more books by E.R. Fallon and K.J. Fallon at https://www.nextchapter.pub/authors/er-fallon

Want to know when one of our books is free or discounted? Join the newsletter at http://eepurl.com/bqqB3H

Best regards,

E.R. Fallon, K.J. Fallon and the Next Chapter Team

Scripted Murder
ISBN: 978-4-86745-815-0
Mass Market Paperback Edition

Published by
Next Chapter
1-60-20 Minami-Otsuka
170-0005 Toshima-Ku, Tokyo
+818035793528

30th April 2021

Lightning Source UK Ltd.
Milton Keynes UK
UKHW041141060323
418101UK00004B/231